BIRD-MONK SEDING

ISBN 978-0-9947104-0-6
ebook ISBN: 978-1-928476-26-9

Deep South
contact@deepsouth.co.za
www.deepsouth.co.za

Distributed in South Africa by
University of KwaZulu-Natal Press
www.ukznpress.co.za

Distributed worldwide by
African Books Collective
PO Box 721, Oxford, OX1 9EN, UK
www.africanbookscollective.com/publishers/deep-south

Deep South acknowledges the financial assistance of
the National Arts Council for the production of this book

NATIONAL ARTS COUNCIL
OF SOUTH AFRICA

Cover design: Sarah Beath
Text design and layout: Liz Gowans

BIRD-MONK SEDING

LESEGO RAMPOLOKENG

deepsouth

*

JOBURG STREET. Noon. Approaching a four-way stop. Off the bus, walking. Wrinkled, close to the bone, legs wrapped in pantyhose with runs in them. Looking poverty-stricken, threadbare sweater, white woman, grey streaks in her hair, middle-aged, as she turns sideways to check the traffic lights her face is squashed-looking, anaemic, seems like no blood coursing beneath that skin. Mouth thin. The traffic lights open for her, and me just behind her. She is about five metres ahead. A taxi, stopped from cutting across by the red light, is idling there. When she is about a metre from the taxi the driver revs hard, it seems to jump, she is startled. I look at the taxi, and the driver is laughing, so is the passenger next to him. The white woman screams, turns to the taxi and shouts: 'jou fokkken kaffir, jou swart lelike bobbejaan!' The bag i am carrying drops out of my hand, an overwhelming rage attacks me. But i can't make out who i am angry at, the crap taxi driver showing his teeth or the wizened parchment-skinned racist creature in front of me. Two Chinese men come from across the street and they shrink back in fear, looking at... me. The traffic light turns, the woman is across the street, still swearing, the taxi still heaves in laughter, i am in the middle of the street. Other cars start getting their hooters going, i pick my bag up and drag myself back to the pavement to await the next traffic-light change, breathing heavily, hot.

BAVINO SEKETE. That is my name. Sekete is 'thousand' in Sesotho. From there to Bavino M. Bavino the Man, I have been called, by friends. Friendship? My aunt's place, 5100 Tsolo Street, Orlando East. I spent some years there. Have i spoken of Vincent Sekete, my cousin who grew up to be one of the Sasol Three, betrayed to death on the guerrilla-front? OK, at some point in that house, lived a family-friend (as they are called). A gentler person i have never known. So shy he seemed to speak from under his armpit. Glass eye constantly shedding a tear. Looked sad. So caring he would advise us not to eat the atchaar from the corner spot, they used uncooked oil in it. Guess what? He turned out to be Joe Mahlangu, the Lovers' Lane killer. Serial murderer. He killed the Romeos & Juliets of the Soweto corners doing the huggies-&-cuddlies. The police brought him in cuffs to the house at some point, and everyone caught a beat-down, even my five-year-old cousin. Cos when they asked where the guns were, Mpho ran & got his plastic pistol. This is how they went into the crime-lands to clean the place up of earth-scum. Muggers, killers, rapists, so forth, even in infancy. We are talking sunken friendship: it has to be a heavy dirge, some kind of 'death fugue', if i were to compose or write that. Actually I am constantly doing it, always, in different ways. I just need to transcribe my cries.

My childhood, well, all friendships I made, came through conflict: brawls, fiya-go, arse-whippings. I grew up in various houses built on violence. But that is a topic for psycho-specialist hustlers and the pharmaceutical mafia to make cash out of. Right now i am talking about this: blood-splat & mucus splatter connections, you could call it. See, without brutal violence, on all sorts of levels, there is no Soweto. I swapped flesh-cutting with fists, running stone-battles, between us kids while punk-arse adults stood there cheering... sick... Anyway, knives cutting through skin. No, i am not carrying my scars in place of medals. Just spitting a little truth.

Talking about unhealed wounds & my cicatrixes that never give up on their itching: this Mark of Cain below my left eye, 5 star is how I got it. My high school mates wanted to run a train, a belt on this girl I had connected with in a tavern. I lived in Phefeni, that night i was in a place called Emndeni, other side of Soweto. Far from home. We went drinking. I met a girl. Street-corner chemistry & the fire-flames. OK. At some midnight-point, this one guy, Thami he was called – classmate & outside-school buddy – he said 'You guys need a stadium?' That is what we call

a 'fuck-zone', a stady – a place for some furtive
in-out action quick & to the point. We huddled,
the girl & i, & came up saying yes, we needed
it. He offered up his parents' backyard room.
Happiness, all good & nice in the neighbourhood.
Hormonal riot coming on, we went there & got
into it, making out. That was the night of my
vaginal circumcision. Odd as it may seem. I took a
thrust, pain shot through my groin, like dynamite
blasting my crotch. Like some razor had gone
slash in my loins. I left the place with blood on
my pants-front & flowing from under my eye cos
then, these guys, friends of mine, came in & stuck
an Okapi in my back, demanding that i get off so
they could get on, wanting to run train. Memories
of shit i would rather drop except to say i got cut,
the one with the knife was trying to poke my eye
out, i think. Well, they too carry reminders of that
night. We all do, hearts heavy with piled-up crap.

Fights: the fluids that flowed on & onto those
streets rendered ties that bound me to others.
The same ones whose heads i tried to lop off, faces
i tried to smash in. We walked off from there
tight, often. But those others are mostly dead,
off their rockers from chemicals braaing their
brains to ashes, deranged drunk, all manner of
freaks & prison-cell hopping. Society's stamped
perverts. Not long ago i was in White City, i grew
up there, as well, and met one of the last of that

number. He was babbling, face grey, hair white, toothless, they take him for Locomotive now, off his tracks... he looked like his own grandfather. My son thought him decades older than me. But we'd run together in torn shorts & sole-less shoes that left our footprints on the ground, showing our dusty toes, same time, once.

I have forever been close to those who do not snugly fit, for whatever reason. In Chiawelo i ran with a boy called BOYKIE, he couldn't speak except through grunts & other non-verbal sounds. Boykie had to go wearing an OK Bazaars plastic bag on his chest cos he drooled, heavily. We would go to Sans Souci bioscope in Kliptown. At intermission get meat-pies, the best this side of things. And half his food would end up in his bib cos his hands were like claws, twisted, he couldn't hold things with any, shall we say, expertise. Anyway, always, at movie-end, stepping out we'd find the coloured kids standing on the stoep, waiting to fuck us up. But damn, after all the Bruce-Lee-Silver-Fox-Angela-Mao shit on the screen, there was no round-kicker better than Boykie. We would hand out free bursaries of arse-whippings & then run off, Boykie shrieking with glee. FRIEND. He would never leave me behind, not once. Guys would not be wanting to hit him, they would be coming for me. But he was always deepest in the fight-mix cos i was there.

At Turfloop the most hectic activist was a guy
without arms, it all ended at the shoulder,
both sides. Always had the hottest siyayinyova
speeches in meetings. All the way upfront in
burning-and-looting time, he'd be shouting
'comrades, thrash this, smash that; no Com X,
leave that one, it is useless, ok Com Y, got the
petrol, right who has the matches...' he was
The General of that barmy army. He would be
organising the running when the apartheid
beasts came. Bad & brave, man. He gave the most
kicks when Varara clashed with Zim-Zim, a sad
pathology that, but... well... always: friend. Never
any sellout detention-moments.

My old man's first stint in prison was a 12-year
bit. What happened, he was drunk asleep on a
bench in a shebeen when he was woken up by
croaks & gurgle-sounds of sorts. He sat up to find
his friend, later to be my uncle, on his back with
a guy wielding a panga over him. My old man,
China they called him for his slit-eyes, got up &
stabbed the guy in his heart. Kaput. They went to
court. Guilty verdict. In prison, asked to show his
number, he said he only pledged allegiance to his
friend. So it was.

Close to his death, Ingoapele Madingoane was a
lonely man. His BC comrades would have nothing
to do with him. But at his memorial the whole

blasted fat-piglet lot of them came out spouting platitudes. Friends.

Peter Makurube died of malnutrition and neglect after all the years he put into the arts of poetry & music. He was persona non grata to all besuited over-flabby frames & business spots. Memorial & funeral what happened, all the rats came out screaming praises. Friends.

Mafika Gwala died torn up, soul cut to pieces but spirit still flying high with defiance & an unchanged, solid belief in what he stood for, a world beyond the grasping, clasping, clawed existence some sold on the stock exchange. That man brought me to consciousness. & at the end there he was in abject dire circumstances. Eaten away with the sickness coming in from without... & then of course the Farts Minister had a lot of broken hot wind to blow about how great Gwala was & that they'd been in negotiation to put him in the education-stream. Lies & bullshit. Faecal-faced Friends.

*

I am here in the bushveld, trying to write an
essay. On Jazz. The links between the Atlantic
bone-rat, the flesh-slash slave-wave-surge & this
south's noises, down the line. I am a dabbling
scribbler and i write, a lot. Of things, and ways.
Forms, too. Straddling the line between poetry,
prose and all that comes with. I put things on
stage. Life's theatre. And in the dust too. Street-
corner and academic podium. No matter. I am a
sentient being, derelict, no abode fixed in space.
Nomad. Hobo.

Jim came to Joburg so Bavino goes to Marico.
Man in the bush in quest of Bosman's ghost.
Finding AWB rabidity. Tranquility so deep it
kills. Hate-hounds. Beneath the surface quiet;
such racist rotten-mindedness. & children dying.
Starvation abounds. Raw sewage in the water
supply. Crap in the taps. Skin matters. Ancient
white beards sexing black teens for tins, food
exchange. The soul's impoverishment. The
starved get their humanity halved. And weekends
of sex-tourism. Alcoholic stares everywhere. Deep
fear too.

I've spent months doing head-work on this thing.
Mista editor said 'Yeah it is great but *no, no,
no*, I think you should toss it all out & think up

another way.' You know, our readers are not, I hate to say this, but they are not *too* smart. This is too, shall i say, involved? ...open it up some more, give it space to breathe. So the reader can sink into it without too much work, you know, I am sure you know what I need, having worked with Bantu Educated people and you so... ahm... erudite... you have to slacken things a bit so they can... get it. They have to get it!'

Mista Jazz Vibe editor asks me to say things about myself, a 'bio' for his readers. Ok, here goes:

Until I went to that bush college called the University of the North to study law the only white people I had any dealings with were my Catholic priest, the doctor at the local clinic... and the policeman. Meaning, one for my spiritual health, the other for my body, and the last to take care of my criminal inclinations, natural since I was bred in a set-up designed to foster such.

The laws of the land said that I could only be born, schooled, grow up, get medical care, worship, have human relations, in a specific area set aside for people blessed/cursed with 'x' amount of melanin. Well, Soweto was and is a slave-labour camp set to the southwest of Johannesburg city. That side of the mine dumps furthest away from the centre of finance (the city-heart). How things lie around these parts is: from the onset, the centre of the city was white and hues got deeper the further outward you travelled. White brown black and in-between, whatever colours played themselves, from honorary-white (talk Asia) to navy-blue.

I was baptized at Regina Mundi, Catholic, by a Father Coleman. Regina Mundi was later to provide shelter, solace, whatever protection it could to the activists who tossed their beings outward from before 1976 onward. That is where I encountered Black Consciousness. The art that shattered my little English-gentleman-stuck-in-the-Soweto-ghetto pretensions.

I got the worst formal education this side of the 20th century. The architects of apartheid, sought to make me and mine 'hewers of wood and drawers of water'. They deemed mathematics, for instance, beyond my grasp. Said it would crack my skull. Calling up butt-bare-crap-faced eugenics, they said my brains were more watery than those of white people. And thus I was unfit for the empirical shit. They said it was 'useless' to have me chained to a school-desk when I could more usefully be out in the fields of the white man digging holes and sowing his treasures, or pulling them up out of the earth in South Africa's blasted mines. At any rate, Bantu education was a crime against humanity, I will say until the end of my days. 'Though my soul be black as sin,' for me... 'baa baa black sheep,' ...you would be hard-pressed to find anyone you could, in all sanity, align to a sheep in Soweto.

I was sexually active by the age of 4, not because, as the craniometer-wielding anthropologists would claim, black people are over-sexed sub-humans, all flesh and no brain, that is, bound to the skin. But rather that with not a single brain-cell-rattling thing to do in that Pavlovian compound, children's bodies turned into laboratories amongst themselves, which indeed they were to white supremacists wielding some power-drunken god's will. And blessing.

June 16, 1976... Hector Pieterson the first child victim of the beast, was shot 200 metres away from the house where I was born, 7758 Ngakane Street – the street named after the man seen as the father of African cinema, in some quarters, Lionel Ngakane – opposite the house of James Mthoba, who introduced 'experimental theatre' to these parts and died some years ago under mysterious, violent circumstances.

My mind feeds on human bits and pieces strewn gratuitously about. I have carried the smell of blood in my nostrils for as long as I can remember. I remember, as a child, saying to my mother that I wanted to be a gynaecologist, and she was proud... then endless knife-fights and torn flesh, skin pulled roughly apart under Okapi and butcher-knife tearing, tomahawk-slashings and the air heavy, wet and warm in some perverse kind of exsanguination cured me of that. Still... the stench of the life-fluids stays with me.

I grew up watching my mother get her face split under the fists and boots of a multitude of men, who, when she (I imagine) could take no more, were pushed on to expend whatever excess anger, energy, fury, fueled by their own emasculation they had left on me. I carry the scars on my back, face, body as a reminder. Anyway... I am here. What more do you want to know?

What more do you want to know?

How, after June 16, 1976, I stood at the door of a gutted bottle store, dressed in slippers torn just so that my toes showed, my nose full of teargas and a case of beer on my head even though i had never tasted alcohol in my life... across the way

was a police truck, teams of uniformed officers-
of-the-gore standing there, throwing dead bodies
into the back of the vehicle. I was 11 years old.

No, scars are not medals. Never should anyone's
art be 'relevant' or of 'consequence' because
they went through this or that shit. Some kid
munching on an apple in some crap American
suburb praying to the tooth-fairy should be
equally valid as a child getting its skull cracked
by mortar fire in Afghanistan, another scraping
and scratching the lice off trying to grab a crumb
of bread in Rwanda and another dying because
some bureaucRAT, some rabid rodent in a high
office some place wiped its arse on 25 million
rand. So too, a couple making romantic love as
some psychopathic misogynist is splitting some
woman's genitalia apart in some hidden corner
of the world. All those are part of our human
experience.

Where do i live now? I am a professional parasite
and an unapologetic hobo. No matter, i carry
Orlando West and all the other places i've lived
in wherever i go. I have travelled all about... and
still, i remain a Sowetan.

I draw inspiration from across the entire
spectrum of the world's literature, fine arts,
music... painters Fikile Magadlela, Dumile Feni,

Lefifi Tladi, Thami Mnyele have always been crucial to my writing. Visual artists with social conscience. And writers who cut out and stomp on whatever literary conventions enslave, from Lautreamont, Artaud, and Pasolini onward.

The South African Blue Notes (Johnny Dyani, Mongezi Feza, Dudu Pukwana, etc) and where they took the music of this land, revolutionising the euro-jazz scene. The Wole Soyinka of 'Ogun Abibiman'. I came to black consciousness via Mafika Gwala. I carry Aimé Césaire in my head. Frantz Fanon is my father. Burroughs is central as daddy formal innovator, plus. That is the company i keep. Reclusive as i might be.

My ghetto-youth bibles: Mtutuzeli Matshoba's 'Call Me Not a Man' and Mbulelo Mzamane's 'Mzala'. Matshoba first dealt with ghetto reality at whitelight, searing, excoriating, burn-the-place-down line-them-up-I'll-shoot-them level. Mzamane made me realise that life grows, even at the most despicable, revolting, down-in-the-sewer-sucking-on-faecal-matter level. My gutter anthem was the ultimate poem of my black consciously-reaching-for-selfhood days, 'Afrika My Beginning' by Ingoapele Madingoane. He died with an axe in his skull, sitting on a toilet. It tells stories, that, about our ends. But life is and will be affirmed, even at the most below-the-back-

of-beyond level. Peter Tosh and Fela Kuti said
they would be here beyond the ticking of clocks.
millennia-long & so far... well, they are.

I was born in Orlando West. Bred thorough
all across Soweto. Orlando East, White City,
Chiawelo, Meadowlands, Diepkloof. I schooled
in Jabavu, Moroka, Jabulani... Even though
homeless, at home. Vagabond wordman. I'll yap,
write, recite, shoot at times, anything to get
The Word out. The Word is paramount. At all
times i walk this land. And talk it, too. My name
Bavino... if Zola-bound, i'd be Kau, elsewhere
Ntanga, or Bafoza, Magenge... Hola Bavino, heit'
Bachana... my Orlando western street corner
male endearment term... & that's the story's end,
when i get on the train at Phefeni station.

At home boko was haram. A vicious evil aunt
thought books bred rats, caused roaches. Put
them out in the yard to be rained on, and
powdered in the sun. My reading became
guerrilla.

I grew up on Scope magazine. The same one
SADF boys on the border worked themselves up
off in order to better rape Namibian children.
Yes, Scope, with its starred nipples and cockroach
legs... the censor with one hand on the scissors,
the other on his genitals... rubbing away and

scrubbing out. Adolescent so it shaped my senses. Grensvegter. Tessa. Die Wit Tier. It was war in glossy pages, on the 'uitlanders'...

My old man peddled marijuana to put me through varsity. Career criminal. Spent more years in jail than our much cosmeticised political veterans. Law is not Justice... check the difference. You want law you go to court. You seek justice you take it to the street. So i hit the tarmac running. I was a guest in dark places I had no wish for. 'I have seen things' the film says... States of Emergency. The Varara-Zim Zim chasm. Zulu Dawn, Student Gang Rapists. What they called 'The Belt'. Tiger balm. Thugs. Pangas, knives, axes in flesh. Bodies crumbling down. People hurt. Blood-wet... I carry the smell of that blood in my nostrils, still. Hits me when least expected... Brains peeping out. Intestines gathering sand. Burning looting bleeding batoned skulls bones broken. 'uLeft uRight, nyamazane'... Lice & lies at police stations. Screech of keys in locks... then the skin-scratch. The stench of inhumanity in prison. Poison in veins, courses brutally, & bursts out, fierce. Bodes well for hell, this. Iyamemeza iAfrika! Amidst it all, my first son's conception (tumult makes the hormones riot).

Eyethu Cinema, midnight show weekends.
Visuals; image and word. Moving frame by
celluloid frame. To be embedded on the walls
of my cranium. Granted it was not skull-crack
intellectual fare. Swords-n-sandals, cowboys and
karatekas. My mecca. Silver and golden foxes.
Then in the middle of it, they tossed in porn. The
censorship hit against the rocks. Titanic crash. To
write cinematic... the poetry of film.

Eyethu Cinema: Mofolo, edge of the reed-lands
and sea-shell sitting there, a purulent sore, warm
inside, away from the hostility & the ghetto.
Temple of some doom, yes; but what the church
should have been also, solace. A place to curl
up in the velvet seat and be wrapped. For the
time it takes for the double-feature to turn out.
Midnight.

Before the feature, the 'showing shortly', what
is to come, scenes cut out, the more fire-flamed
turbocharged designed to hook, like heroin (oh,
Bird, that wire cut deep into the system, right
thru the mouth and out the anus... and it could
not be pulled out, the day they tried... it had aged
you twice, and when it plopped out, so did you)
from some next week future... to tell 'come again,
what's coming is better maybe than you are about

to see'... and then... splashed across the sea the
ocean, and speedboats and pretty people on them.
And helicopters, and adventuresome others trying
to do the yummy ones in... heartstrings pulled
and of course at the final moment, our beautiful
attraction-worthy ones coming through and
then... 'Peter Stuyvesant', the main man striking
a light and necklacing a cigarette inhaling in
time with the female sighs in the audience... &
'the international passport to smoking pleasure'.
Then the big, rugged & tough Marlboro man.
The virtues of machismo. Battling the elements
and coming out winning the beautiful women. &
then to wash the mind all clean of dirty thought,
Lifebuoy, the red coloured 'soap of champions'.
Moving images of the soccer dribbling wizards of
the day in their glory. Percy Chippa Moloi, Scarra
Sono, Kaizer Motaung turning defenders out.
Sport, the thing of aspiration.

Sans Souci. The coloured beyond black factor.
Meat pies & sticks & stones. 'Julle fokken kaffirs'.
Fights in the dust, battles to scrape the colour off.
To get to paleness. & days, when moneyless, the
proprietor sitting us children on the stage, the
screen a metre away, looking up. The figures on
screen all jaunty, twisted out of shape, the guns
all wobbly jelly. & then outside, after the film, the
coloured factor. The kicks to the stomach and you
would be holding in the meat-pie you ate earlier,

trying not to throw it out. And the swollen eyes
and the dust rubbed in the eyes. Yes, sand to
your sight & there is burning in there. And Bruce
Lee, Silver Fox, Golden Fox and the Shaolin
Temple is in you. And you stand there. And they
are yellow around you, and you remember how
Mr Ma-Kick jumped up, turned around, twisted
& flicked his foot at that crap villain... and you
tense, clench muscles, & take off & spin in the
air like you have seen... and just then the one kid
had come away from the rest to hit you when you
were not looking... and you smack him square in
the face with the inside of the foot and he takes
to the dust mouth open and he gulps on the soil...
squealing. & the rest see that the martial artist
has stepped off the screen into the streets of
Kliptown and you dig deep into your lungs and
let out a yell straight out of Hong Kong and the
Kliptown bully-kids take off in all directions...
and you are a hero striding home, until next
weekend when you come back, and your friends
slap your back and Boykie guffaws into his OK
Bazaars feedbag.

& then later, all grown. Vietnam in celluloid now:
Platoon, Apocalypse Now, Full Metal Jacket,
Deer Hunter... ah, power playing with itself.
Even when heart-tearing intestines around neck
screaming out injustice decimation genocide
holocaust it was always about The Power. The

Vietnam Ho, Nguyen is nowhere to be felt. Seen perhaps, fleeting as last week's rice in the paddy. The conscience tug, the questioning, the vile inward-going and outward spew... all American. Vietnam just a canvas to toss vomit or kiss-saliva at. All films of supposed conscience just American ejaculation like when the porn comes in between the features, to kill time so when the last film ends the sun has broken. Then we can go home through the reeds with sight enough to see the muggers and night-time marauders lying in wait... yes, when the skin bits come on & there is tucking at meat in the dark and the juices fly & land in the hair in the seat in front... yes the gore, the blood & the bullets eating through bone and sinew... & all the while we were screaming & shouting hoarse for the Ah-Mary-Fucking-Cans!

Eyethu Cinema midnight show. One intermission, a neighbour, chair next to him empty. As the lights went out a woman came, slid across the aisle, a bag of popcorn and a paper-cup. I saw the man had his elbow on the empty seat, fist clenched, facing up, she sat on it. Slight wet sound emanated from the contact. Heavy sigh, i looked away and at the 'showing shortly' flashing across the screen. And shortly after that the Peter Stuyvesant commercial (pretty people in speed-boats and private jets flying across my famished imagination)... that is how i started smoking.

Eyethu was uterine. Warm and liquid in there while outside the wind howled across Mofolo Park, carrying cries with it. & the barks of order from the down-low demanding either money or life. Today, at home with cinematography, i sit in wonder of the censor's snip and snap, thinking: 'none more graphic than lived reality'.

The Omen – the devil child come to lay god's kingdom flat in his father's name.

Swords n Sandals, togas – Brad Davis, Dan Vadis, inhumanly bemuscled top off & in what looked like tablecloths, carting swords that made the air scream in soprano, slaying slavers.

Spartacus & the ten gladiators – the ultra-muscled super-he-men.

Boris Karloff – maggots growing out of one side of his face. The side he'd previously lain on, in his grave, before the rising.../resurrection-blues time. He'd flick those maggots at the enemy and that was that, a torturous death.

Woody Strode – sole blackman anti-hero. Or perhaps Sydney Poitier, clean-cut and pasted in dignity. Looking good. Once upon a time in the west. He died within minutes of his ebony prettiness and shaved skull getting us all black

powered each one to FIVE FOR HELL – scary
Klaus Kinski encouraging the wearing of scowls,
the masks of emasculated Soweto life.

The Unholy Four, that number against a fascist
army. We went blasphemous, sacrilege was a
thing of love. The magnificent seven. Yes... the
numbers kept coming.

And then... The East comes to town – Angela
Mao, swordswoman – the cure for gender violence
had a name. As she slashed thru carriers of
'powered' genitals.

Johnny Robot – Japanese (i fantasised myself
with this gargantuan steel-fighter, super-
human...none would touch me. But all my friends
died violently.)

The west is here, Valdez is Coming, Death Rides
a Horse. Terence Hill and Bud Spencer for the
comic factor, My Name is Nobody. Lee van Cleef,
Clint Eastwood (not acting, they said, just fitted
into the frame) – Man with No Name, heroes to
the nameless. Or the deliberately misnamed.

Film brought me here. A brutalised child, skin
flayed off my back, week-days the torments of
school, sadistic teachers who insulted, beat and
gloated, and then the 'after-school is after-school'

threats of others licking mucus off their Dracula-snouted children, i got from film some kind of distilled knowledge. Experience heightened and capsuled for my exclusive benefit.

*

In Johannesburg, Moferefere Mehlolo is a
pharmacist from the dumps. He is the one who
made it out from beneath the garbage, worked
himself out from beyond that end. From the grime
of his near-existence in this wretched place, from
the slime-clogged sewers he hacked his way out,
tongue-first. To the fore marched his intellect. Up
& away, first of anyone. He comes back, often,
finances some students. His older brother was
artist. & comrade. Friend. Got his little brother
hooked on the word-works. Then the brother died.
The only person Moferefere felt or, was close to,
or loved. He was devastated. A lot carried its way
into his being over the years. Pushed, he schooled,
came out tops. Made cents writing assignments
for his fellow students. Genius child. He came
out of campus & was snapped up, dodging racial
knives, by pharmaceutical companies. He hates
them today, says there is a conspiracy to kill him
because he has exposed their nefarious ways.
Still, he thinks heaven of me.

Then came the night Lehlohonolo got stabbed
with a surgical scalpel. & the music stopped.
Backtrack: Lehlohonolo is a hip hop MC of social
conscience. Great consequence. A serial verbal
innovator formal stylist. His music saved me from
a nervous breakdown, on two occasions: Central

Europe putting glass to wrists. & then i played
& listened to his lyrics. They were ropes pulling
me back. To firm land. He calls me 'father'.
Says my writing carried him forth, from days of
uncertainties. & the resultant identity searches.
Crises of self. Much black love coming down the
decades from all sides. Two young black males
locked in brothered celebration of an elder one.
Then the knife-flash like fratricide.

Long story short: Moferefere came at Lehlohonolo
with a surgical scalpel because he detected
disrespect. Offended he had called me 'grootman',
saying 'why call him that, do you know grootman
means a baboon'. Then he cut him up. & the
shebeen queen took centre-stage shitting me out
of her establishment. Pea-henning among the
drunkards, queen for the night, first time since...
blaming me... because he 'came here with you, i
saw it' & i hung my heart out. & haemorrhaged.
I did not see Moferefere leave, but you could
hear his war-mobile high-power cough in heavy-
rev, throat deep, sleeked to smooth flow breath.
Turboed up right to its veins, & plane-march
away. Meanwhile Lehlohonolo's life-juices were
flooding up the floor-tiles.

I went up to the shebeen queen, my walk tear-
charged. She was sitting on a couch, the level
low. So i had to kneel. & try tell her my hurt.

She not once looked at me. Her friend, next to
her, spoke. Saying how i did not even witness it
happen. I had been talking poetry with another.
But the queen, all eyes on her, was wallowing
in the relish of it, my persecution. I got off my
knees, they were hurting anyway, walked away.
& no longer wanted young talent around me. &
revoked my shebeen-licence.

& that was when i hit the road, bushward.

*

In the playback it's the calluses on the
percussionist's palms that haunt. Kind of
drumming that hands out concussions. Stop-starts
bowel movements. Echo-chambered it becomes
'shadow of a mirage'. Auditory illusion, sonic
phantasm. Knocks the cranium until white dust
comes out. Talking African drum & the bass hum.
Deep earth moan calls up soul in dead skin, rotten
flesh, calcified bone... 'give the drummer some!'
comes the Brown command.

The lamp comes on with a brightness that blinds
in my head. Last day, darkest cloud forming,
without and inside/ like death is walking over
here. And life wants to get out, into the world. & i
sit. Gather thoughts together like scattered rags.
Grab pen, seek paper, find scraps torn out of old
school exercise books, look at the bookshelf off to
the right, a rustic bookshelf, some dead farmer
had used as a pantry affair to store & display
mampoer on, confiture, the bible, and ancient
prayer books. A lurid, dabbling child's attempt at
water-colour painting.

> WAT IS 'N HUIS
> SONDER 'N VADER

In block letters on shimmery blue, pink, grey.

Framed in brown borders. TWO BIRDS in same
colouring facing off and across from each other
like swords formed in mortal duel, hostile.
The painting is boer naive. Reaching out to a
nationalist god getting lost to the teargas in
the heavy winds. The water running down my
face burns. Napalm must sting like this. Agent
Orange. My veins are deranged, standing out
thick on my arms, glaring like they are going to
burst. I saw a man shot in the face once, with an
assault rifle, from close range. It was like you
could see white-yellow maggots crawling in the
red there. From deep where his madness once sat.

Here in the bushveld shebeen the ferment takes
hold in different ways. When the ethanol hits,
Sis Betty gets delirious, starts telling everybody
who will listen her life story. 'Beng'muhle mina,
in my days i was the beauty around this place,
you can ask Boy, he used to run after me like the
horny dog he was. I got all the men on heat when
i was around, they will tell you. & even today
you can still see it. They drop my name as far as
Joburg, these guys. They talk about me like there
is no other. They say drop dead & thrash around
gorgeous me... and now'... she breaks down
crying. Aesthetic pleasantness of the past pulling
on her tear-glands, & the horses in those depths
start galloping.

& Bra Mafisko. He had his legs shot in the old days. The hospital amputated both of them above the knee. He drives a car still, though, automatic transmission. An old Ford Granada. He sits sideways, a walking stick in his one hand, pushes it onto the accelerator to get the car moving & switches it onto the brakes to stop. His taking corners is a thing of beauty. Better than the show-off young thugs in their BMW 325s. They call that car 'ithemba lamarhumsha' (hooligan's salvation) because if a guy is getting chased by the police through the streets, his only prayer is to get behind the wheel of a 325, no other, because once he slides in there & gets the key in the ignition, they could barricade the streets & pull out the entire police service, there is no way they are going to catch him.

They lean an elbow out of the driver's window, cool in the breezes, cigarette in the corner of the mouth, better yet a zol. & it is class, driving. BRA MAFISKO is megastar of that. No one can look & pose better at the steering wheel than him. & in the shebeen he sits there, his pants-legs stopping just above the knees, tucked back & held in place with safety pins. He handles his brandy glass like an aristocrat. & talks about the days of his car thieving. Holds court, glories gone coming alive in his face. & it is wistfulness you see there.

Then there are other drinkers who, when the waters flow, throw up the Satchmo in them, and nothing will stop them from singing. In the far corner where the shadows are deepest, sits one who walks funny. Drunken to vomiting once, the sick calling the rats, he had his feet, thick black with toe-jam, eaten by them while he slept. & here too are ones whose drunkenness makes them remember god. & they quote the scriptures.

My grandmother used to do that, hit the bottle & then get the hymns lubricated. She'd start preaching, to no congregation, or the unwilling among us, who had no ear for the righteous. & then she would sing into the night, you'd hear it float above the wall easing to a metre from the roof. It would start high, sonorous, with the angels twinkly-toed inside the verses, and then as the night wore on, their wings drooping, they'd tire, get their legs wobbly under them, until they came flopping down. & in the end her voice would turn into a whispered sermon. Then fade out completely. & then the snores.

In the shebeen now, these others sing, out of tune, some. But there are others, Maria Callas sweet, Nina Simone soulful & getting honeyed even more with the liquored reinforcements. & then, as the minutes tick on, the saliva starts crawling out of the lip-ends. & they go incoherent. There are the fumigators, trying to quieten the noise of the cockroaches flapping their wings in their souls, to drug them to sleep with the fumes. The ones who breakfast liquid & carry it into the night. The Kippie Moeketsi descendants, who blow on their air-horns & invisible-flute their way through the hours. & then there are the criers. A few sips & they get saddened. Mournful. They snivel, sniff, & the bawling starts, out from dark places in their insides. & of course those whom alcohol turns into everybody's lover. I sit there and watch. & the abject poetry of it all jumps into my head and takes me over.

'I hit him in that blasted face of his that looks like someone took dynamite to it, just below that air-emptying nose of his and above his snout, & my fist came back with a mucus-streak so i punched him again to clean it, to take the nose-drip off... & then i kicked him just over his donkey dong & i can tell you he will be pissing blood for a month, I'm telling you i left his bladder punctured like a balloon, it was like Legs of Thunder Sikhosana just took a penalty...'

On the benches along the grime-encrusted wall, sitting under the speakers fastened overhead, silent now, everybody wanted some spice to their own stories. A woman was saying, between gasps of air, for effect, pretending to be whispering, but making sure it was delivered like from a theatre-stage to the wings: 'She got him bewitched with that ancient cunt of hers. I bet you the cobwebs she has in there have him believing she is a virgin when everybody knows even the Madikwe river baboon has had a piece of her... sies.'

And across the room, leaning against a stack of crates full of empty bottles... 'Talking about witches, they call that stuff Black Science, you know? But here is the story. He walked with me all the way to my gate and we were yapping, well i was talking & he was just grunting & laughing funny, & i know i have jokes so... anyway, all the while i thought he was just a dwarf, this guy. I mean even when my woman opened the door, looked down at him & for a moment stood like a statue, eyes jumping out of her head & running away, & then screamed like she was giving birth right there and slammed the door so hard i am still looking for the wood to fix it, prop it back onto the frame. I didn't get it, i just thought she was drunker than i was & swore at her. Meanwhile this guy was not just some small man wanting talk, it was a thokolosi, you know, some people's creature of the night...'

The hiss came from the speakers then, like a vinyl plate had dropped in the juke-box, snatches of jackal talk over it... 'I was just in

when she said oh wait. Pull out let me get in
proper position, so i staggered back & stood there
swaying, so drunk I was, waiting. The juices
holding onto the head. Next thing she took off
through the door, running... her auntie came to
collect the damn woman's panties the next day.
She'd left them right there, on the floor, in the
middle of the room, can you believe it. But you
must know i don't play with this thing, man. I
hit it so hard smoke comes out of it. Auntie said
she had to come because the woman could not
walk properly. I said oh yeah and i gave it to the
auntie, hard; she is grown, that one, she could
take it.'

Cackles... canned sound coming to drown the
talk... 'Well, me, the other one, did you hear what
she said when she saw me, the only thing she
could get out was 'hm, wena' and she could not
even look at me, she was so ashamed. And then
she snuck away like some stray raggedy black
cat, did you see? You know what, i caught her in
my yard the other day. Midnight. Naked. Just
standing there, staring at nothing. See, i couldn't
sleep so i went out to get air. & there she was.
Standing transfixed like someone had superglued
her to the spot. You know i have tightened my
house, mos? My traditional doctor does not play
games, he goes up to the mountains & under
the water, he is strong that guy, don't mess. &

you know they say you must not speak to them
when they are caught like that, like mummified?
She was bent over forward so i did not have to
do anything like position her or whatever. So i
just whipped my piece out and stuck it in hard,
very deep, my friend. You should have heard her
shriek like a demon had its tail on fire. I worked
it in & out & you could have sworn i was stabbing
the fucking life out of her good & solid. & long. I
splashed & drowned that kitty and then i let her
go...'

The nitrogen kicked in from the juke-box, bass
distorted, zero tweets, the midrange insane.
Things are not rolling if the music is not hitting
against the cranial walls, inside. It has to make
your intestines shift. Decibels running in the
red. & only then is a party going on. Otherwise
it is just a white people's tea-party convention.
Dunking cookies.

The Dreamer Artist Activist is here too. He was
brutally tortured, some years ago. The after-
effects of it have stayed with him. A patchwork
of variegated, ill-matched, navy-blue being
dominant but with brown & off-white plus some
black in the mix, layers laid as with uncaring
hand, & holes cut in at strategic point for orifices
– that is two different-sized, flaring nostrils
winged at the ends, eyes, one of them ever

opened at half-mast. Mouth with lips larger on the left than the right side, the lower jutting out & curling over the upper, and to the side, ears, the left with the lobe gone to leave a dead slab of wrinkled flesh hanging precariously, like some thread holding it against gravity. All this makes up what could be called his face. He used to be a pretty boy, before he went 'inside' & emerged looking like Leatherface's wet dream.

I had him over to my house the other day. He was drinking like drowning something ugly inside him, gnawing at his soul. Sadness overwhelming, too powerful for anything else. & the hours dragged on. & it got too late for him to stagger home. I made bedding for him on the floor. Two blankets for him to lay on a pillow & then another blanket to cover himself with. We sat talking: 'Nobody can hold out forever, i don't care how brave you are. The nerves break at some point & you will beg them to let you talk. & tell them even things they never asked you about. The crocodile clips on my balls, man... the electric shocks, i think they burnt something to ashes somewhere inside me, man. There is a deep something in me, i tell you. No, i am not ashamed, i talked. What wakes me up screaming at night is that... i pissed & shat myself... while they watched...' and he sobbed, softly.

I could not look at him. & then he got under the
blanket. And curled up, foetal. I sat there for a
while, then stood up to turn the light off, and got
supine in the other corner, opposite him. Time
passed & a smell like a mosquito crawling up my
nose woke me. I sneezed and sat up. The light on
the stoep came in dim through the curtains. &
his squatting figure, not a metre away, was there,
head bowed. He was grunting. His hands on both
knees, eyes shut tight, in the grip of some dream
he seemed trying to break out of, squeeze it out
with all the strength his bowels could muster,
defecating onto my bare floor. A massive load.
He sobbed, in broken baritone, his tears running
down the drainwater pipe, in my ears.

His face is skin-pieces put together with staples.
Not exactly Frankenstein-monstrous but...
he is the ultimate ORGANIC intellectual. No
patronisation though... not institution-like.
Talk hip hop scholarship & the academy thinks
saggy jeans, gargantuan tasteless heavy neck-
pieces like Burning Spear remade by Third
World chanting 'we must pull it... with shackles
around our... ' yeah, forked wood either side the
neck-piece slaves in a line & rope around the
neck claiming re-appropriation. Slavery Days,
the tune. 'I can't breathe' busting a platinum-
mounted verse through the arse must give you
stomach-ache... ahm...

*

Bud, electric-crackle emotion-bound. Max... in Bird-flight solos deep & high on the melody tip. What wrong could Bird do but lay a harness on that and ride a horse through it all... going out on the course, composition tucked tight under-arm. Baptised in sweat. Thus it is i find self-place in the Yardbird Suite. Jazz Hotel. This music is passion. & like sex it comes draped in perspiration.

'It is as important to know when to play as when not to', said croaky Miles.

'Let the music breathe', spoke the Blue Notes Moholo.

Mnyele's master-piss was no urine but blood corpuscles. & the fart collectors came. Yes, spurted & squirted hard cos it was beyond ink, pen, charcoal & the canvas was a man's skin. Blown up, later, to pieces in real slime. No slow motion. MEAN IT. Minute. & mean it is you say it. No con, scam, hustle. MAKE IT REAL.

The place sits in its own grounds. A duck-pond, fowl run. At the entrance 'clever' signs painted white on blackboard:

Kom eet Of ons vrek Albei van Die Hongor

Warm beer Cold Food Bad Service Come See
for Yourself

Free Beer Topless Barladies False Advertising

Husband Daycare Centre – leave him with us –
only pay his bill

Home is WHERE you keep your Beer

Soup OFF the day BEER

And just inside & before the restaurant-bar
itself, a structure stands in brown bricks & wood
banisters, black painted railings, chairs on the
veranda around wooden tables, rustic scene.
Other tables in the garden, in front of the pond,
benches on both sides. Just in front of the well-
kept garden, razor-edge cut lawn & a painted
rockery. A sign there, also:

DRIVE CAREFULLY

We only have ONE hospital & two cemetries.

The veranda is a metre above ground-level,
where the garden is. Stairs lead up. Old white
woman, wrinkled, small, in a yellow & white

summer dress of an era gone, wants to get from
the stoep to the duck-pond, looks at the stairs,
decides against, & walks across to the edge of
the stoep, stoops. I'm scared she'll fall & break
something, looks like she's on the verge of
cracking, crumbling, anyway, at the very least
turning to powder. She puts her arse down on the
ledge, her skirt hitched up high & above decency.
She starts dragging herself forward, pushing
her little weight along, her path pushing the
dust on the floor off to the sides as she passes.
She is not wearing panties, her legs are splayed.
Thigh-skin showing like scrambled eggs. I know
what Champion Jack Dupree meant. Just folds
of faded pink & pale & in the centre hairy grey
surrounding. This is the bushveld. I blink, fast,
a few times & clamp my eyelids tight. Turning
my eyes away. I feel the vomit rise. I am being
blinded. Deliberately. She is looking straight at
me, turning her genitalia same direction, sliding
on forward & off the edge of the stoep. I turn
quickly away again & keep my sight away for a
few seconds. When I turn my eyes again she is
standing where the lawn starts. & hobbles off
towards the duck-coop in the corner where the
lawn ends. The bile rushes into my mouth & i
stagger my way to the toilet. My guts hurt. I will
not eat. I carry myself on out. Past the graffiti,
red on black, on the wall alongside the N4, red on
black: SPERMLOAD KILL.

The bush stretches here, packed tight, it carries
far as the mind can go before dropping down
breathless. A hawk seems to be swooping to
strike. But no, it is falling, plummeting down,
lands on its stomach. Wounded maybe. Or it
got too old up there in the polluted beyond
and carries its disease here. The bush goes on,
inexorably. Inexhaustible, still, even as the
without impinges and intrudes. And comes in
without invitation. Unwelcome and hostile,
bringing with it mirrors.

No, the bush does not want to see its own face. It
might force its sight within, to the soul festering
in there. Maggots dancing in a fury hell would
be envious of this. There is a heavy hate in the
air here, hate and heat mixing in a noxious stew.
It covers the surface tranquility in blue-green.
Worms and fireflies when the sun goes down. And
the shadows come out like ancestors laden with
the wounding of history.

The township is a scab on the landscape called
Seding, off to the side of the N4 freeway, the scar
cutting through the bushveld, to other times
and places the bush tries to shut itself off from.
That road that disappears beyond that mountain
range that straggles like an obese sprawling
obscene gymnast, in the distance. A smaller sign
of an old injury rests across the road. Cars pull

in there to feed. Filling station. And off to the side, ten metres away, a bottle store. Parents, grandparents and their teenaged children dot the grounds, khatuns of Tlokwe before them, as the sun beats down.

And talk: o ja mang ka pol-rekere, *who are you screwing with a cock-rubber* sies o ska ntlhanyetsa... nyo ya gagwe e nkga tlhapi... *her pussy smells of fish... don't put your madness on me... what will you do for me black as me? Go and die no difference yes i will kneel before the white at least he can make me live you just poverty fuck you.*

And a lodge just behind it, made up of a few thatched-roof chalets. Across the way, mornings and afternoons, people walking with bales of wood on their heads. Harvest of what the bush rejected, tossed out, threw away, vomited out.

*Across the broken waters... King Sunny Ade takes
to the road heading to the House of Dub. Handing
out digits along the route. A map leading out.
'That's my number', declaration like gang
affiliation identification.
Man home-bound, dome a bag full. At burst-point.
Sounds in it.
Blazing atmospherics like breaking out of the
prison of petrified aesthetics.*

BABU owns lots of property here. Nobody knows
how he got his money. He came here a while ago,
in beat shoes and frayed pants. He was selling
revolution to the populace. Babu was an activist
for the party before it became government. He
was conscientising the black ones. The Afrikaners
do not like him too much. I have heard them say
so, even the liberals. Anyway, he got a road built
that leads past the township. That was when the
settlement was still all shacks. Before the tiny
mortar and brick structures sprang up as part
of the 'human settlement programme'. And then
Babu built the filling station with the restaurant
attached. Eyes wide, people watched. And now
Babu owns land on which he has packed wild
animals: buck, zebra, ponies, miniature horses
on the one side, along with cattle and goats.
Demarcated with a fence on the other side he has

set up a 'Predator's Camp' (so says the inscription
at the gate), a lion has been heard to roar,
sending the houses along the ridge rattling. It is
said that he is trying to get a tiger out of India.
He has wild dogs too. And other killer animals.
People believe all that came as payment from the
ruling party for having got them votes.

THE SEWAGE-SEPTIC TANK VAN always
hurtles through the streets. The stench of it
hanging in the air long after it is gone. The driver
seems to be trying to speed faster than the smell.
Hoping to outrun it. I wonder if it stays with him
when he goes home, dug into his system. It is a
smell like thick, heavy death hanging in the air.
Babu turns the corner of the post office, looking
across to the butchery with 'Deutschland ueber
alles' in graffiti against its wall, strokes his foot-
long beard with a manicured hand while keeping
the other Swiss-watch steady on the leather-
covered steering wheel & headed in the direction
of the police station, the library and municipality
offices. German engineering tells him all is fine.
He is plush in cool comfort outside the hard harsh
tired & hungry thirst-laden bushveld sun, the
Merc speaking to him, lulling him. Massage of the
senses.

From the opposite end the brown-striped white
truck speeds with SEWERAGE scrolled in black

along both of its cold drink tin-can shaped sides –
the reason why children shouted 'coca cola' every
time it careened past. Trying to take flight off the
ground, attempting to escape its own stench, it
comes on, a predator of the road, snarling deep-
throated in menace. In the fine interior Babu sits,
waving to all he passes by. Man of the people.
Politician personage. He got them voting, didn't
he? And look at him now, they love him for it, for
the brick houses where once they crawled around
in corrugated iron hovels. They are grateful,
aren't they? They have pay-per-use electricity
now. Soon perhaps the tap-water will run less
brown.

& then the impact. The truck hits the C-class
Mercedes bang on the nose. Metallic intercourse.
Miracle of invention. Screams in the street. The
truck skids, slides, carries the Merc on its bonnet
for a stretch of road. Crunch-time. It seems to
hurl it back, both staring each other down. The
horse, simple faced, ugly even. The cylindrical
trailer, all brown-streaked white with black
writing. The trailer groans, coming apart like the
tailoring was going. And then brown fluid starts
oozing out. From the sides, the back, the tin-can
coming apart. People cover distance, fleeing. Like
it was blowing up. A splash of faecal matter.

The drunken man sitting on the pavement tries

to lift his hands to cover his nose, the limbs will
not move. He makes another attempt, fails,
shrugs and just sits as the sewage reaches him,
sneaking into the holes in battered canvas shoes,
rising up to his ankles. He stares, in hypnosis.
No baptism to be welcomed, however the heaven
promised. The trailer creaks, stretches and
sheds exactly half its length. Heaviest and first,
the smell, no longer constricted, released from
bondage, sprawls. Invisible pall covering the
streets. A child vomits on his school-shoes, people
gasp, the drunkards across the street paint the
ground with vomit, and what they throw up
moves to merge with the contents of the truck. A
mass-mess. A deluge of brown black yellow green
solids swimming in sickly liquid... and then, in
the middle of it all, that sewage, the corpse of a
baby. Foetal. It seems to move, ever so slightly,
borne in the urine & faeces mix. Babu stares, eyes
wide. Shockwave upon another. The truck driver,
higher up, gawks too. Mouths open to scream and
gulp down doses of weighty putrescent stench.

SAMPOKANE is the night-soil-man locked down
in Setswana lore. Feared. No bogeyman, him.
You see him, each dying day. After you've dug
heels in, moved bowels, purged, dropped the filth
nothing about you wants, wrenching it out of the
system, the rot that makes you shudder to look
at, that your nose shrinks from the smell, that

you want no part of you touching, that disgusts
you should the tiniest piece of it stay stuck to you.
The essence of death, in all senses. Sampokane
thrives on that, lives off it. He comes to collect it,
takes it away, out of your presence, far from your
sight. Sampokane subsists off it. After that what
could he back away from? Sampokane will kill
and eat it. Whatever it is. SAMPOKANE is scare-
walking.

Thus it is that Sampokane the faeces & piss-man
& Babu the political animal face each other off
above the human waste reaching out to climb
up their car tyres, hoping to sneak in to them...
above the carcass of that unnamed baby in the
middle of it all. & the sun comes screaming
down, & the fumes rise, the smell hits hardest.
There can be no amen to this from where i sit, a
metre above it all. The smell of it hits me down
to the stomach & settles heavy enough to keep
me seated. Eyes on the scene. That dead baby
looks like it is smiling at it all... Fear turns to
hate. Mass feeling. Communal. Cowardice turns
murderous in numbers. From beyond the street
the sounds of excitement fatten themselves on the
hoof. People come splashing through the effluent.
An old man trips on his walking stick and lands
face-first in the sewer-mix. Opens mouth to grunt
in pain and some of it goes in, he scrunches his
face and digs broken-nailed fingers in the filth

and lifts his frame, with all pain draws one leg up
by the rickety ankle. Then the other. Sits down
in the stench and ugliness. And the numbers
run around and past him, to the two wounded
vehicles, and the baggage of human waste and...
infanticised times.

Thus it is that all advance on Sampokane. To
force him to EAT the dead baby. Only the two
men, Bra Joe Sejabana the Elegant & Maswejana
the Pretty Playboy stand against it.

BRA JOE. The Elegant. Barefoot. His feet have
developed thick elephant skin. Crackled, heavily.
Some dried out river. Drought-stricken. Furrowed
much. A layer of dirt-black creeping up from the
back of his heels. Unwashed. The sweat, dried
up days old and still packing layer upon thick
layer up, oozes off him. And in all this, he oozes
something unnameable. The aura of the man
is diamond-to-forehead brilliant. The tattered
shirt, its tails flapping as he walks. No, he hops, a
caterpillar on the street. Spasmodic. On invisible
springs. When he sees me he pretends not to
notice me walk on by. At the last moment springs
out in front of me, hand out, palm pointed up,
and mouths in an incomprehensible tongue...
never loud or clear, rather a deep gurgle from
yesterday's throat, from depths out of sight. Often
i drop coins in his hand. Soon as i do he hops on

off to the butchery down the road graffitied with 'Deutschland ueber alles', disappears within, is gone for a while, then emerges munching on a stick of biltong. If not the butchery then the Pakistani shop up the road, for loose cigarettes. The smoking of which is a ritual, a show of class. I've seen him sink down onto his haunches, sigh, strike a match, light up and... smoke. Cigarette between index and thumb, other fingers flung out in limp-wristedness, cocked like bourgeoisie handling wine-glasses. The other hand on the other cheek, lost to the world. Cigarette up to mouth, deep drag, smoke held, then released in calculated exhalation through the nostrils, smoke rings too. & i have wondered, never known what had led to this. Middle-class mannerisms in the dust. Time to time a fling of the left arm, a flicker of sleeve to wipe off stray mucus, then back to the cigarette.

Bra Joe is friends with MASWEJANA the Pretty Playboy. They say he was a ladies' man, Maswejana, in his time. Now, not yet in his middle age, he walks down the streets, eyes staring, but at nothing. He is always clean-washed, clothes ironed. But his mind everywhere but here, in this time, this place. His one ear is drawn, like a cartoon character, a few inches out of sync with the other. His face tapers down, egg-shaped, mouth forever puckered, an eternal pout.

He drools a lot. He is coherent, though. Speaks,
can be heard, but the understanding is elsewhere.
They say he was the hottest chicken around town
before this, dressed better than any. Township
lore though has it he disappointed a woman
he was to marry... and ended up like this. Just
woke up one day and couldn't put his face back
the way it was before he went to sleep. His right
leg started shrinking, centimetres shorter than
the left. His left turned inward and he couldn't
hold anything with it. His one eye, the one above
where it should have been, forever streams tears,
constantly cries. A sign of his remorse, they say.
He walks around, grunting, looking at nothing,
but sees enough to ask me for cigarettes only,
never money. I stand talking to him, spinning
stories, jokes. And he takes it in. And laughs. And
when girls walk by, regardless of how they look,
he says: 'ba le maswe jaana', as ugly as they are...
and that is it. 'You owe me, no no no, man... pay
me now, when are you paying me?' I say i have to
go home and fetch the money i owe him, i will see
him later. & he tells me he will wait until i come
back.

Days they sit together, Bra Joe and Maswejana,
legs straight out on the floor, next to the only
ATM in town... smoking, conversing in tongues i
cannot understand. Emotionless. And they stay
there for hours. And the world goes by. And they

watch the dust, maybe, and its people blow on by. They pass a cigarette between them, smoking each in style, after their own special manner. And they seem lost in whatever dimension. Or space. But locked together in some understanding. Mutual. It's a sight for wonder. And when the odd ATM-user saunters by, draws money and starts walking away, Bra Joe shoots his hand out. And the day goes on. I have seen the laughter on their faces sometimes though. Like they knew things i didn't. No one else could comprehend.

Thus it was on the day of the crash, when the sewer-septic truck and the political-activist-grown-affluent's Merc collided, that Bra Joe and Maswejana threw themselves in the mix. Babbling incomprehensibly and in furious indignation against the sewer-man being forced to eat the dead baby. The only people in the mad mix to throw in their negative, lashing and kicking out against the crowd which brushed them off. And as i gauged my beliefs against my life's worth, something solid whacked into my head.

*

The rock against my skull beams me back to
childhood-street in White City. Standing there
and the crowd to sides and back. Upfront looking
down i see my first love, little sister of my friend.
She lies there. Half her body, the legs on the
pavement, upper body leaning, sprawling out
and bleeding, into the street. Her blood draining
out and away down the street to the storm-water
pipe. Her head, the part that meets the neck, has
lifted off, cut away like abandoning the rest of
her. Taking flight, off and away. It is like a panga
sliced in deep. I can see, in the midst of white,
brown, the throat pipe slashed through, it blood-
spurts at intervals. I love her. I stand there. The
wound is so deep, sharp and eating away that her
head is swung far forward and onto her neck... i
stand there all of 12 years, the big toe of my right
foot showing through my wet canvas shoe and
scratch at the skin beneath the patch on the seat
of my pants. Her big brother weeping next to me.

Bra Vusi, he was a professional soccer referee.
Friends with my mother and her man, Dr
Mabinda. The doctor was a veterinarian. He
worked at the People's Dispensary for Sick
Animals in White City. PDSA. But on weekends
and after work people would come to the house
with their ailments and he would treat them.

He'd write out letters for those who needed a
letter to prove to their employers they had taken
ill and could not come to work. He made a lot of
money, the doctor. The children around the place
would look at me with envy in their eyes because
my life was beautiful they said. We lived at his
house. & we used no ordinary soap to bathe, it
was some fine smelling soap called Dove. It was a
beautiful house inside. We'd never had furniture
like that. And the food we ate... Ah. But... he beat
us, often. He split my mother's lips sometimes. I
grabbed his leg once when he was about to kick
her while she lay on the ground... he hit the top of
my head with his fist. A red light came on inside
me. Then he kicked me in the stomach... i woke
up in the dark. Much time had passed. He had
two sisters, nursing sisters... they always saw to
our wounds. & would say soothing words.

Bra Vusi always came on weekends after the
soccer matches, to sleep over. He bought me my
first bed, a comfortable one i could really sleep in.
He was a gentle person. He always came around
with his lady friends, the two sisters who lived
two streets down. On this one day the doctor
slaughtered a cow and had the neighbourhood
come for a celebration of something, I do not know
what. And Bra Vusi came too. With a woman
friend. Things were fine. People ate. And danced.
And sang. Then an old lady spoke nasty words,

saying the doctor did not know how things were done. There he was, she said, standing there eating, even before all his visitors had filled themselves. That was not the black way, she said. Some laughed. The doctor had not heard her, if he had there would have been trouble. But things were good. And then later... after the eating, when some people were preparing to leave, i do not know what caused it but the doctor began beating my mother up. He hit her on the side of the face and she fell, and hit her head against a rock. & kicked her in the stomach. People screamed, shouted. Some men tried to hold him back. He was fearsome. Bra Vusi came running from inside the house. He had been playing records on the turntable, making music. He ran to the doctor and caught his hand as he bent down to hit her again. The doctor turned on him. Swung. Bra Vusi ducked and spoke to him, i couldn't hear him. The doctor swung at him with his other hand. That is when Bra Vusi hit for the first time. And again. And again. And then the crowd closed around me, i could not see. When they parted, the doctor's face was a mess. Of blood and bone and broken flesh. His front teeth were gone. I saw that when he spat the muddy-dirt that had formed over his lips. He looked horrible. The shape of his face had changed. His eyes were swollen shut... the people left. My mother carried him in.

The sisters had not been at the feast. They came
the next morning. Just after my mother had
finished cleaning the doctor's face up. There was
much talk in that house. And the sisters had ugly
looks on their faces. I was sent out. Bra Vusi had
left after the beating, taking his friend. We were
alone... we were alone again, me and my mother.
We took our things and left. Just two plastic bags.
All the beautiful things remained behind. We
walked a long way from Chiawelo to White City,
my grandmother's, that day. And the heat was
heavy.

＊

The police come. Big and fat. Slugs dragging
their bellies. Authority-riding. Arrogance
powered by cowardice, hiding behind the shine
of the almighty badge. They take Bra Joe and
Maswejana, the two 'mad men', into custody.

The police here hide from the SEXCESSES, and
Alsatians used as rape instruments. Numerous
cases are reported of farm workers forced to
succumb to fucking the baas's dogs. And other
farm animals. It scares them. No case number for
that. They tear up the statement right after the
complainants drag themselves on the tail of their
shame out of the charge office. The overwhelming
number of bestial instances goes unreported.
They can go to church on Sunday, happy in their
station, protectors of the law, defenders of the
weak. On Monday baas drops milk off at the gate
of the police station. And they grin and lick their
lips. And baas walks off happy, vindicated, his
milk is sweet, he knows, he sweetened it with his
semen.

Forced sterilisations on some farms around here.
Abortions performed in barns and agter-kamers.
The Madikwe river-bed is baby-corpse lined.
Foetuses float on the waters, some days. The
water here is said to be the best, country-wise. It

feeds the outlying areas. Botswana gets its water supply directly from this river. The flavour must be brilliant. It is all in the taste. The township's water passes through the reservoir in the middle of town, by the time it gets out and into the pipes it has changed colour. And content. Mainly the discharge and excreta of other, less melanined humans.

There are many light-complexioned children around the township. And still, the talk around is they are curbing the growth of the numbers. People are dying in distressing numbers here. Odd diseases doctors cannot or will not disclose. AIDS is the blanket strewn across them all. There is talk that people on the farms get injected with things no one knows about. And it happens mostly with young women, and men who are 'problematic'.

People point at this white man walking down the street. Last year the police begged him to put his gun down. He had been sitting on the hill opposite the freeway, with a high-powered rifle, taking shots at minibus taxis passing. A lot of them went off coughing out blood and with bullet holes in their sides. Inside them, shattered heads and much blood on the seats. Cries. The police came, and spoke to him like a person needing special attention, a child with special needs. They put him in a police van and drove off. He strides across the street now and black people hug the corners until he passes.

There is a training camp some kilometres into the bush. Some days khaki-clad trucks and 2/4 trucks head out there, from wherever, carrying white youths waving guns out of the windows. Readying for civil war. The message comes out to 'move west, like our ancestors... it is time to take it all back...' In the fields towards the freeway, bodies are found, some mornings. And to the back of the town, across the rail tracks. Nobody searches the farms, so nobody knows of the corpses become manure there. And yes, the northwest is prime beef country. No meat better than to be found here. Much of it is human. It is just never said. The meat piles up in the abattoirs, the butcheries, the chisa-nyamas but the cattle numbers shrink next to nothing. Good farming practice, it is called. Farmers Weekly sings praise, every issue.

PAULINE. I walked to her farm, 5 kilometres outside town. I had stayed there a few times when i first came out here and was looking for a place away from that soul-polluting city i am cursed with calling my birthplace. I went to collect my book of poems she had asked to read, she wanted to work a piece into a song. Tranquil, the walk, cool afternoon, the trees ruby & rosy-cheeked. All well with the bush-world. I got to the place, the sun leaning over. I heard the low moans & the high panting just as i was about to knock. The door was off its latch, unlocked, slightly ajar. I pushed it open and it swung in with a bare sigh, as of a wind-push.

Her huge figure was on the kitchen floor, flat on her back. Her maxi-skirt that she normally wore when she strummed her beloved guitar and mournfully sang to the gathered tourist audience at the Bushveld Poetry & Song Festival was up and over her chest, up to her chin. Her eyes were slitted, her cheeks heavy pink, she was all sweaty and breathing like an asthma attack. Her thick thighs were open, her knees high, heels rhythmically pumping up off the floor and down, in time to some rhythm i couldn't hear, until the slurping sounds came through to me. Between those thighs, its short penis-head showing while it jerked its back to & fro, her dwarfish, shaggy dog with the droopy ears and heavy stench, was working its tongue in and out of the hole in her middle. That huge vagina parted, liquid, and closed as the dog flicked its tongue in and out. Her husband was an electrical engineer who lived in another town 60km away. In that moment, holding my breath, i thought i understood. Neither dog nor woman seemed aware of my presence. I turned to slink away. As i touched the door her voice, heavy with passion and forcing its way out of that massive body, said: 'Wat soek jy... wil jy 'n gedig skryf?' I crashed out the front door, her laughter, harsh & shrill, unlike the one i had heard in song so many times, ringing in my ears. It stayed with me all the distance back and into the gathering gloom.

*

Softly soft step into my hard times
Come in smooth into my rough life

I am the tsetlo-watcher. Witness the hypnosis. In
the power-greed death-game.

Old socialist-communist-comrades gone capital is
like THE YEARN. Ultra-straight man on crack-
cocaine sticking massive phallic objects up his
rectum when the rush takes on. & Gael said:
'It makes you know the truth about yourself. It
is a serum. Gets you paranoid still, and you go
scared of even yourself. Your shadow tails you,
stalks you, talks menace to you...' The sexual
exhilaration is without outlet though. Builds up
to explosion and then just peters out, leaves you
whimpering, it is majangling electric-wired like
the brain cells will explode, and you feel them,
on the burn, the ends going to ash. The ultimate
white-lit end of it just beyond your reach, and you
grasp, your nails wanting to tear out even, if the
need arise... and you try a hold on the nothing
out there, just... outside your grasp... your arms
not long enough... always just micrometres away,
you never get to it. And know that for truth but
no matter, you have to... so you hurry up and
light up away before it disappears forever, you
think... but inside you is knowledge of how vain

it all is... and that even if it were not and you got to it, you would be smashed to bits, what smithereens means... and that will be the end to miniscule you in the universe floating up there before coming crash-landing on your being. And still you want it. And the hunger makes demands like starvation is your all.... and just one bite will be your salvation. IT IS MASTER, YOU ARE LESS THAN SLAVE NO RELATION MORE DEMEANING.

But you must obey because your genitals will it, the crotch reaches out, desiring deep. You want to fuck to the end of the tiniest crevice. And the biggest juice-dripping orifice beckons. And you want to squeeze the extent of your very self out of your body, it is a casing you don't need anyway. You need your obliteration in the pleasure promise. So you stoke up white, open the coils. And the glass-pipe hums, mocking. And the rock sizzles and opens its legs for you to come in. Penetration time. You clutch the lighter tight. Don't want it running away and gone. Need no loss now. And the seconds ticking seem centuries... and you flick and flame up, trembling in anticipation. You torch up, and solid turns liquid turns gaseous and your inhalation makes it shoot up your tunnels, seems running in and out all your holes. Like the hair is in shock standing up. Hold it in long as the lungs

can withstand without collapsing, coming down
hard. Joyous like nothing else ever since time.
Hold, keep it in, still, blow out, sigh. & the wash
comes. And baptises and blesses. And the warmth
floods. And you grab your cock and pull. And it
is to cry... it comes closer. & cums inside you.
You pump harder. Fuck images flash, dance in
your head behind your eyes and a million pussies
yawn wet hot open and you sink your skull in
them, all of them, same time. And you feel them
wrap around you. You are your cock. And cunt.
And arse. And sucking mouth. And sucked.
Cunnilingused & fellated to all sevens. And still it
calls you and you're staggering. All the while you
are running on your haunches though, like your
legs amputated above the knees. Hard as you
gallop can't get there. Just on the point of coming
it fades. & it is back to the beginning. Of your
time, your existence. You tremble, shake, shiver,
collapse into yourself again. Spent. And you did
not even ejaculate. The call comes again. Seduces.
And you realise your eyes are closed, so you open
them and stare. And the black green yellow red
stars exploding behind your eyelids retreat. You
flop down defeated.

They come, the bourgeoisie, the 'made-it', in
their fancy clothes and over-fed bodies. They like
nothing better than to hear the starved say 'thank
you' for the crumbs they flip off and flick with

manicured fingers. Makes them feel affirmed. Regardless of how much of it they consume each moment, they need it some more. They don't ask 'for more', they believe it is theirs to take. The Yearn burns. Inside the German limousines, within the uterine folds of the 4 x 4 luxury SUVs, the capacious BMW beasts, the Merc Benz monsters, the luxury animals enfolding them in polish and shine. They don't see the misery. Or more truly, they see it and rejoice, makes them know how far off the dust and away they are.

Mrs Nation-father, after her husband died and fresh from London exile, took her adult son, well into marrying age, on a drive to the edge of Soweto, stopped the big car just off the freeway and opposite the mine-dumps. The ground bones and fine-sifted flesh out there stared. On that hill, clear day (like Sitas spoke of about class struggle), the view was panoramic. And off the side the blonde tour-bus stared out too, and the feeling was zoological garden. She looked across smoke-hung Diepkloof to dust-roofed Orlando as the sun set, its rays trying in vain to cut through that pollution. It was a sickly yellow-golden as she asked him, his Kente-clothed figure over the silk vest caressed, the pearls on his buttered wrists jingling, the struggle heir groomed to perfect fit for the throne 'Do you see yourself marrying any filthy diseased thing from over there?' flicking off

an Italian shoe and the French perfume rising
off her armpits as she pointed long, perfectly
manicured fingers at that slave-labour camp.
The diamonds glistened in the gathering gloom
off her fat fingers. The blood-soaked bits in the
diamonds, you couldn't see, shining deep deep
within the green blue within, the same colouring
the blue-green like Baas foreman looking from
above the shafts, content, consenting. Leer off
the spitless mouth-side. Glinting in approval.
Reclining in over-stuffed couch-satisfaction. Put
your ear to the ground, something the bodyguard
would kill you for trying to do, you could hear the
dying screams rock-broken, limbs twisted at odd
angles, boulders cracking the rib-cage to free the
punctured lungs, sharp-stuck. They say pigs bleed
best. No, go down the mine. & hear the bloodsong,
gurgling like pipes gone mad and taking over the
psychiatric institution. Even the rats flee before
the flood. & the life-fluids spurt, bursting out to
promised freedom, drowning out the voices fading
to croak above frog-level, but one limp-lotioned
hand's dismissive flick and it's muffled. Censored.
The heir grinned, like it was joke-time. And
the car purred, u-turning and off to affluence's
northern suburbs.

The stars come out to play in the bushveld. They
cavort, tossing light and tickling the trees. And
when the wind blows you can hear the trees

giggling, happy. Very close by. It lubricates and scents the senses. The breathing bush whispers its happiness. You feel like you want to touch the sky deeper than Hendrix. The firmament seems like it wants to touch your eyes and it is wondrous, especially if your whole life was tied to the Soweto-imagination-prison habitat. They smile, those stars. & the moon comes out seductive-like, wanting to wrap around you. 'Ah but your land is beautiful' once said the dreamy wonder-struck liberal. He didn't know the cursed & poisoned half of it.

*

Free bopping. Re-bopping. Be.
But Miles walked on just uppers. The soles were
his feet's, not rubber. That was left stuffed in the
mouths of the dead Congo Belgium colonised.
Plantationed in a partitioned continent. And
set alight. & then Lumumba's pieces no glue
could put together, to make The New Man. &
Mobutu Tutued the west & they wrapped him in
a corruption-free vest. Saint to the Profane... blow
horn.

Bushveld dawn bird-orchestra. Deep growls,
horses-n-trailers in the freeway distance,
growling changing down. And then off into the
Botswana-bound distance or back from there.
They pull breath in and out, shake heads and in
satisfaction, or bad mood, depending, go on eating
up the asphalt. Road-graze. Predatory, still.

Tiny community, Seding. The country's smallest
municipality. But the regularity of graves opening
up beats average middle-town. You see it in the
expressions walking. Always on the verge of
waking. And never doing it. Just going through.
Doom walks here. Hangs on the shoulders, a
monkey clinging tight. An air of resignation
surrounds.

'All we have here are our bodies, and they fade.
First goes the elasticity under the constant
pummeling, the hammering, the getting beat
down. They shrivel up each day, get turned
inside out until the red parts come out to the sun.
Then no grip remains. And without that, what
is woman? So you cannot earn by it, then... ' She
looks earth-beaten, jaded is not a description.
Standing by the freeway roadside sticking her
thumb out at passing motorcars, but only the
ones with the sole male driver. Or the ones with
no female occupants. She is going nowhere but
to the end of a negotiation. And back. And then
again. Just a ride to some sweat-laden rustling
paper.

She is hitching flesh-sales, she tells me. Just
open-faced. Poverty does not know what shame
is, she lets me know. Morality is not edible. No
destination except perhaps a pot on a stove. If
that. 'And the children shall eat.' 'I will shovel
shit if it will feed my seed.' That is the wish but
often it is first, and then last, a frothing plastic
mug brimming with potency's brew. Then,
perhaps... next the children will hunger-stare. &
she will beat them, accusing them of being spoilt,
they ate last night so why the tears. And then her
man will beat her in turn. And sleep will come.
For all.

Freight train, driver black, in dark glasses
though the sun is not burning down yet. Cool like
that, leaning against the door as he scans the
landscape. Relaxed in the caboose. The carriages
rattle down the tracks and the earth shakes,
feeling it, minutely shifts, stretches and eases
back. On his cellphone, or making a show of it, he
waves at the early morning over people waiting
at the trackside for the vans and trucks that will
take them on day-contracts to the surrounding
farms. He gets his siren going in cheerful greeting
and there are whistles from the ground. Grey
metals chugging down. Easy in his character. The
earth shakes in good nature. The train goes on
and under the bridge in the far distance and...

... DAYS GONE, of my childhood. My big cousin
Kenny would at dusk grab his overalls and leave
the house. His friends standing outside the yard,
waiting, already clad in blue overalls and boots.
They would go around the corner and a hundred
metres down to the bridge between Orlando and
Kliptown stations, jump over the little railing,
slide down to the tracks below and wait. & the
goods train would, minutes later, roll on down,
and stop. For supplies and fuel. For water and the
energy-matter to be got at the coal-yard across
the way. The coal to be loaded on a horse-cart
and driven down. & the workers shovel it in. And
while that was happening Kenny and his friends

would have the padlocks bobejaan-spannered, bolt-cutted & crocodile-pliered off, clip the padlock's ears, slide the steel doors sideways open, and jump in. A wealth of goods in there. In minutes in the carriages, choosing and throwing out whatever they fancied in there. And on and out. And no one hurt. The Afrikaner driver and his guard, coffee from the coal-yard in hand, all supplies retrieved, would get back in, start up and be gone. & the township would buy what Kenny and his band had to offer.

It went on until the train-guard, on one occasion took a walk down the length of the train and surprised them. A heavy-set, powerfully built, red-necked, bush-bearded man, put up a fight and got his head split open at the end of a wheel spanner. Jail-time ensued. And when Kenny came back out the goods-train was no longer stopping under the bridge. The bushveld black train-driver cooling it in his dark glasses and easy manner puts the question of change up in my mind. & somewhere in my depths a sad river stirs.

★

SCREAMSCAPE. A MAP. & a dog litter riff.

'Even my dog is smarter than they are. I tell it to
go fetch the sheep. It goes, it gets them, it lines
them up. And into the kraal. But them, they are
stupid, all bloody baboons...'
'Oubaas don't call me a baboon please...'
'Yes you are an orangutan... like the rest of your
people.'
'Well, but oubaas knows it is oubaas who is more
hairy than a monkey's testicles. And pink like the
head of its penis... so why is oubaas...?'

Oubaas exploded. Came at him swinging with the
whip. Thano knew he could take him on. He side-
stepped the first lash and stood watching him.
It was at that time that the rest of the workers
jumped on Thano, holding him down, hard. One
put a knee on the small of his back, and he felt a
bone break. 'What... you want to fight the white
man, hm? Who are you to stand up to... this
man... putting your hands up like that, what, you
want to break oubaas' arm...' & then things went
black before his eyes.

The farmer owns this world. The farmworker
died, it was not baas's fault. Laziness deserves
all it gets, even if to be wetted with waters from

within. What if the man was too weak to take it like a man, like all of them, why was he special? It was that skin. Not made for it. This is a hard land, it must be harsh. They survive who are equal to it, even the animals know. He got his tools, the ones he used to skin the cattle. A cow was much more business, not this. Easy. He could do it in his sleep. He had, anyway, dreamt this kind of thing, many times. He cut the body up, in the moon's silvery glow. It glistened cold. Like the hatchet and the butcher's knife. And the hammer to drive the chisel into the joints. He cut up the pieces, taking his time. Swearing the dogs away each time. He packed the bits in little clear plastic bags. The next day he would take them to the Bosveld Butchery. They paid well. When time came he would tell the family the man had run away, like all kaffir men do, from their families. What was new?

They had been lifting the brown bottles and cackling like tinkling glass down in their stomachs, from the look. 'I took him to the fried chicken place there, and when i turned around he was chewing up the bones, the white people staring at him in disgust, the one child threw up on the table. So i took him out quick and we went for ice-cream next door. Bought it through the window and i was still greeting the guy in the apron and when i turned my man had eaten up

the ice-cream along with the paper wrapping...
damn, i am afraid of starvation, the things it can
make you do...' & the circle laughed, holding its
sides. I went inside the shebeen. Inside one was
saying: 'Ok so you got a fine behind, and then,
that your talent? See me, walking on water, that
is nothing. Forget shark and piranha, want sushi,
i'll get you that to go with the bread...'

REQUIEM: Civilisation carriers set humanimal
against manbeast. The chains rattle in the
colosseum. (& Mafika died, impaled on wood-
stake Hammarsdale & the government that had
rejected him affected an undying affection pose.
Professed love, the kind that kills.) Blood beats
down on the gladiator head-splitting, watermelon
open. Flesh on meat-heat. Blade-flash cold to cool
it. Cultured applause from beyond the barriers.
High seats throw down perfume in buckets into
the arena, the kill-zone, to drown out the death-
scent... then go out to legislate on human rights.

*

& In the slave-sound air laden crackling tropical
storm the singing Louis
Armstrong was the U Roy's voice-swing on the
flying beat. Thelonious Monk kept
turning around on the spot babbling silent. & Lee
Perry swung around & over
again same spot arm out in chant. & it all came
down... to the same. coming over
AMERICARIB soundwavelengthwise.

ART, BIRD... no other course than to go opposite
the public's direction.
Marrying content & form, what I need least is...
acclaim.

Bird, face to his demise, reaches out for a Jesus,
says: 'save me, Diz'. & that is... Jazz.
BBC says that's a slang word for sex... oh, BANG-
noises.
(some of its creators hate the WORD.
Davis says 'call it Miles Music', same Miles fired
his Sting-historied bassist 'cos
there were no silences in his playing... no open
spaces.
Same time Miles said Bird was a hog, Trane a
pig, so too Rollins, oink-colossus on
the saxophone. Interpretation: Mark of the genius
is... porcine.

McCOY. Both of them the real. Tyner, Mrubata.
Horns to keys, & both sun-kissed.
In brutality's own equation, the one lost his
daughter to butchery,
otherside the laughter: music's own treachery.
I wouldn't barter one for the other. Cos facing the
overseer-financier public, it is
easier to compromise your art than release a fart.
Still, some play the piano of
flatulence. & others the sax of tummy-runs. This
language for me... is neutered.
Trying to put the sex in it... jazz it up.

DIZ. White dance. White dance. Piano at
intermission. Then the toilet call.
Coming out a man with a bottle got his blood
drawn. Uniform turned crimson.
Big bad beer bottle in hand Diz says he was
'gonna crown' him. But band-hands
held him down. Bird cursed the guy called him a
'cur'. Diz found fun in that term.
Diz of love, care & battle... i, too, am going in
RED. Cos Diz bled on the record.
Left bone-particles in the vinyl. (before things tail-
spun out of control.

'It will take a long time to combine my loosely
hanging thoughts'
– Tha Hymphatic Thabs

You can't write in the modern jazz idiom without
noting a debt to BIRD.
I misquote, but it is for the Improv-factor of
things... on the established.
Polyrhythm and complexity of harmony. The
Parker legacy, sir. I am heir.
The base was there before me. Solid. I stand my
pen on it. And the paper winces
while i wait for the blood. It is where i take it from
there on in. Going
stratospheric with the grounded. Down-beat street.
Step. 'the melody's more
important than the navigation.' And motif is
trampoline in this. Bounce on it
only to take off and then back again... on the one!
The idea though is to take it
away from the inherited form. Make a new dream.
Four-pronged attack,
channeled through one. Mafika Bird Monk & Me.

House, they call the music. My eyes stray to the
shacks. Incessant, monotonous,
thump of canned programming. I remember once
LKJ saying when dance hall
sounds moved from live-band instrumentation to
the CASIO drum machine it
pushed the sounds closer to the streets, gave it
more dust, rendered it evermore
organic. Creak &... a sandstorm hits the
shackland & i avert my gaze. Tension &

release the metallic walls expand & contract that
percussion instrument, the
tube with sand in it, you turn it around & the
sand runs down to the other side.
Still, the jukebox goes ballistic. Tinny, whinny,
ceaseless acoustics slap to the face
and the crash of a cymbal. Jah bless the
synthetics.

Purgatory blues like urgent bowel evacuation
needed
but a butt-plug is propped-up deep & solid in the
rectum.
Sand hitting the sides of the mkhukhu sounds like
Mongo Santamaria thinking
coral reef meets tide coming in heavy. Santeria-
soulful. Wave of sound. Hell,
sheets like Trane-tracking biting down on his
dental pain. It shooting up to vibe
with the Heroin withdrawal one week into his
solitary-confined-to-water-diet-self cleanse
before the Ascension.

The Caribbean meets the Arctic coming on spastic.
Identity plane-crash. Melt-flesh.

*

I mini-bused myself three suffocating, sweat-filled
hours to the JOBURG VILLE. Expensive dressed
in poor veneer. The face slum, the core bourgeois.
Bars, restaurant, bookshops where upward
mobility gets its chops. Tattered jeans. The
designers charge more for the holes and patches.
'BRAKE. Break your fall & CLUTCH' sign at the
filling station opposite. Designer poverty too, like
bringing illiteracy's scars to seminars.

City built on bones, blood, flesh... its haunted
avenues pretend ignorance and blame the past
on the present. Dipping tea in the cookies. The
water flowing uphill... 5'o clock afternoon swelter,
clammy, sweat-filled. Heaving paper-bags &
hauling up plastic sacks. The colours darkening.
& the sweat flowing heavenward away from it all,
the service and toil. Breath-heavy the taxi queues
snaking, no... tortoise-moving. Around corners
of the downtown & trodden-bound. Hugging the
smells of oriental spices, the sweat of armpit, brow,
crotch, & between toes turning black jam, fabrics...
& cooking. Restaurants grunting under the weight
of last week's food recycling, and oil used over
and over 'til it runs thick black trying to shed its
own weight... the blinds about to go down. Queue
marshals holding court, lording it mighty over the
commuters. They can afford it, no options out here.

Passengers hostage to taxi-drivers' insecurities
played out as macho-man rules... Never nowhere
more expletives, colourful sexual references
swearwords anywhere, than taxi-world. Take
my holy word. Kingdom of the knave, this. In
the exhaustion, the torpor of it, the deadening of
the long travel after the long slog and the trudge
around where food should be... and the snivels,
the tears, the... aaah... but the children, ah, the
children... for now though the wait.... the years
gape, up ahead, a grave. And behind, the decades
yawn, bored. Even as they swallow. And lick lips
afterwards.

And opposite... the stock exchange opens its oiled
orifices and dislodges, from deep lubricated sub-
terra bowels it discharges venereal... from uterine
parking lots... Lamborghinis, Ferraris, Porsches,
never south of here... BMWs, Mercedes that
never will touch dust where uncoiffed humanity
walks. Per capita never nowhere. And the queues
sigh. Eyes on the moment. The convertibles glide
past. The SUVs lost in urban slick growl with
all leisure, inching away & the masses' stares
are dead. On target. '4-4' shout the marshals,
pushing the lined up, chest-heavy, buttock-
weight, thunderous-legged, squeezing them in to
minibuses. & driving past, the monstrosities of
affluence, wealth own show-reels unfolding on the
screen of the urban streets, licking tarmac... they

exude airconditioning, warding off the heat and the humid in things. The queues get their cool by proxy. Comfort by association with the street. What is osmosis? Rub up, might get some. Not in the eyes, looking out mocking, from behind tinted windows. And the street & queues watch... & then momentary lapse, miniscule movement in that affluent direction... then realisation bubble burst disappear... truth is... deflation. STEP.

BEFORE THE COMING we capitalised BLACK. And that is the colour he was burnt. Truly. No, blacker than that. Like the car-tyres and petrol set alight on humans. That black. But before that... when the first brain-drop fell on his arm he looked at it, it was his. & he thought the rain was falling yellow now. & when they repeat it they laugh. In the street. Still, the other one, skinny humpty on the metal wall, the performer for toil-drunken applause. The top-of-the-train dancer, the train-surfer... he misjudged, got his takkie caught under some steel railing on top of the train. Couldn't dislodge himself. & when the electricity hit him... above all was the smell. The power-cabling sizzled. On Phefeni station platform people wrinkled their noses and thought of boerewors. The aroma of human braaivleis they smelled. Memories of Vlakplaas.

Walking down the street and a voice behind me

says 'heita' and i turn around with a 'hola' out of my mouth and the figure, furtive, shrinking away, a man says with shame in voice 'oh, sorry, timer' and i feel old, punctured, but then again... walking down the street in another place a different time and youths in the street greet with much bowing and scraping and 'ah, greetings uncle', and you smile at the respect and return it to them but then a moment later realise... they were looking at your pants, to see how far your turn-up was from their hands, and what speed they needed to lunge and pull them up and you sailed or flew or swung or staggered up into the air and the one grabbed you by both legs before you hit the ground and the other turned your pockets and they laid you right back on your feet and walking again, centless... in the street... like you had taken no detour... and your head spun and the blue yellow green black stars came. And you turned and looked at... well... nobody – they would not be there. Gone... long gone past whatever corners you know... and, if that way inclined and your anger and fear did not stand in the way, you would have to marvel and chuckle at it all. And say yes, if that was the class they displayed, they deserved your money. And walk on by.

The POPOMALA people, i have seen them nod off, go off and asleep on their feet in the middle of the street, standing among people, sitting on the floor... they go off totally, completely, out of consciousness. And remain rigid, standing or sitting. Minimal heroin, rat poison, marijuana and who-knows-what. They take a toke. That is, prop the pipe up and light up, suck it in deep, hold it. Tight in the chest burning to run out, keep it in, hold it... and when nothing else but chest-crack remains, let it out... and then... the lights don't blink, they blow out. Dead. The man could be drawling out a thing, some coherent bit and then... out. No warning. A heavy kick it gives, that. And later, minutes, hours... they don't know, when they wheel back in, the light explodes and he is there, present. And the system starts gnawing at the nerves, the senses, and it calls for it. It eats out the insides. It wrings the innards, it pythons itself around the veins, constricts the nerves. And IT has to be got... so... 'uncle!'... eat dust.

THINGS beautiful hip brimful of life, they mass the streets, upright eyes future-ward, even in revelry sure... how many destined to go prostrate at destiny's dead feet? No answers here, i turn the corner. Page through. To read more of this booked life. I push myself through the thick, acrid air. Life begins with excretion, nothing pretty there.

They drop out of protective vaginas running to

get their smarts calling their mothers whores, tramps, sluts... mouths smutty off venereal discharge. Yes, they are man-loving, 'my niggers before bitches' but turn butt around tight-clamped talking homophobic. All that after they lip-gloss with semen.

They burnt plastic onto the head and shaft of his penis because... well, the child lied. Said he had been touching her... 'in front' and 'down below'. The more he screamed the angrier the crowd became the more afraid she got and... so, the more she lied. Scared they would harm her if they knew she lied. So they cut off his penis and put a condom on it, set it alight. From the bottom of the shaft up. It burnt climbing. Went out at the head. & someone said what remained was a black mushroom. All laughed. & she still lied. & laughed too, then.

For them rice & peas
For us lice & fleas

*

'Should i go for the smoky Dizzy mix OR
Lucidity?'
'No, no Lucy Ditty... bring the core, hard.
Not the plastic wrapping. No paper-rapping,
either, messing with classics mixing them with
wackness...'

'Check out Charles Mingus – radical activist
super-huge trooper personality short-fuse & the
match close to ignition-tempered social conscience
deep-earth on the bubble-music, & the lava is
political engagement...' i say to the one carrying
'beats for the muddy-mix' in baggy-jeans & the
wheels-of-steel plus the one with the golden mic
and the platinum lyricism, mapping their route to
the hip hop battlefields.

Then i spin the disc & there's not furry flurry
showing ego-laden off like 'look, ma, i can play!'...
plus it's not always i go with BASS-slaps (love it
too much for the violence... unless it is "Funkie"
Mohapi's Humnana... i hum it deep behind the
beat... whiplashed from facing the woofer-air
blasting my bowels... just a little off & pressured,
a cough that will be suppressed no more. A release
i would rather NOT want... some wipe their sweat
off with human skins.

The gathered, sweating, angry-to-trembling Afrikaners in the dusty street want it to have been an attempt at rape. An assault on their grasping at white nationhood. The hands are on the guns. The trucks roar, eager to grab whoever it was. Old woman speaking, the one who lives in the house opposite, with her Parkinson's-diseased geriatric husband who can only hobble a quarter step at a time from the door to the gate, and her divorced, middle-aged, bulimic daughter. She speaks fast, her squeaky voice trying to rise above the deep-throat growls of the trucks and their old-republic-clad occupants. She prattles fast about how i am a good person, i live in that little house behind the trees, i help out... and it is to have them not turn their murder-intent and fire-attention on me... Yes, they gathered in, wanting it to have been an attempt at despoiling this white woman.

And the victim... she struts, the attention bringing a little colour, in vain, to her face. She is walking off her soles, bouncing, glad. She looks like crumpled khaki, like brown paper wrapper out in the elements too long. Like she has been through storms, wind, dust then drain-water drenched and cast out in the driving sun. Pink blotched some kind of symmetry across the face. Deep lined, the visage. Trenches cutting in and across. Thin to the bone, you can see the bones

sticking out on both shoulders, desperately
holding her shirt up. She bathes in the harsh
light of her victimhood. For a change because
always when she walks past, the boers look at
her. Surreptitiously, the grimaces forming, and
steal their glances away, never staring. Ashamed.
She is no boeremeisie to hold up in pride of the
Van Riebeeck and oom Paul Kruger old tradition.
She hustles all – black, white – for money in the
street. The pale skin peeling off her face. She
collects and sells scrap metal across the freeway
and... you need not be told but you can see the
drug-hunger. The craze behind the skinless eyes.

This day her two children, 6 and 8, ran screaming
down the dirt-street and cries filled the air. I ran
out. And heard through the trees bordering our
properties my AWB neighbour furiously saying,
loud-voiced – i later learned it was into her
telephone – 'kom gou... kom gou' and blabbering
incoherently, other things. By the time i got to the
gate there were three trucks and a couple of cars
gathered in the street, guns on show. A police car
arrives, and the police are bored, one yawning. It
is Monday morning. They don't believe this rape
story. The AWB neighbour, predatory, like the
smell of blood was in the air and the wounded
close by, was wafting and floating around, holding
centre-court.

Through the babble it emerged: he tried to rape her... it was 10 o' clock in the morning... middle of the untarred street. And the street has pedestrian traffic. Workers walk the street in their overalls. In their numbers. Why would anyone try a thing like rape in the middle of it? He tried to tear off her clothes... he pushed her onto the ground... yes he ripped her shirt... But the shirt is intact. And the beasts are gathered. And the two children whimper... He was trying to take her phone. The faceless nameless black, trying to steal her cellphone. They want it to have been an attempt at rape.

Let the jazz be free, Ornette Coleman came and said. And then did. Set it thus: 'Not interested in mastering forms or styles others invented. / Originate. Innovate. The creativity markings...' as the prose colossus looks at the page while Sonny Rollins caresses his horn, blowing off the bridge & into the wind. Better that than rubber-stopped senses.

The serial killer with the ideology against white supremacy targets white women only. The Ideologically Inspired Serial Killer – white woman, the last bastion of racial supremacy – preservation?

'The black woman is at the bottom of the food chain... oppressed all about by the white power structures, by patriarchy... her own man... the white one held up as the ultimate... the measure of aesthetics, everything spins around pleasing this fake, elevated, supposed to be treasured angelic whose sex, even, is used to sell dreams. The racist, xenophobic cry "would you let a nigger fuck your sister?"... shit, like she is some fruit on a tree you could just pluck at your will and horniness like... without freedom to decide whether to do or not... some inanimate object just waiting there for brother to give the say-so for

the knobbing... damn, i wouldn't want her but
still... the power behind that is... yes, she is seen
as the one gate to the impurifying of that race...
so... well... if that was so... I was going to smear
the kind of filth on that canvas like they wouldn't
stand to look at it...' Pink femalehood, the last
bastion of Aryan self-worth and supremacy. The
anti-miscegenation murder squads have castrated
Black Male going back centuries and to the
future... endangered species, Mista Black.

So Serial Murderer goes out to level the splaying
fields. No sex, he finds it disgusting with The
Aliens, as he calls them. Says when the lies stop
floating, the blood too will cease. He has cut up
four and going for six when they catch him, the
boer-brigade in khakis preserving the purity of
their whiteness. 'Serial Healer', he prefers. In
a sick land. The newspapers palpitate, as can
be expected... his technique: reaching for the
deep hate, he eviscerates her then puts a wheel-
spanner in the wound, heaves to let the innards
out jammed – cell barred, he calls it – in the rib-
cage, to free the 'hidden Black' within. A kind of
lumberjack. He says also: 'They are scared Black
man will fuck you so you can't walk? I would
not dick them if that was the only thing to stop
my cock falling off... i got myself an industrial
stapler, i ram the labia, attach them to the thighs
so they can freely spout all those race-lies without

that politically correct mess of human righted
hate speechified censorship... i let loose the
bigotry excretion... let your pen screech on that.' I
take note.

My cousin Vincent Sekete went to bring The
Fire. He and his two comrades hit Sasol,
Voortrekkerhoogte, Sasol again... & when they
came back again, and hid in their safe house...
THEY, the South African Defence Force,
surrounded them. In their numbers. They had
been TOLD. By HIM, the National Hero, leader
of the liberation forces, the armed ones, where
the three had sprung from. The animals inside
the Kruger National Park rioted. They smelled
the blood, & the cordite. They heard the death
screams. The Sasol Three laid the land for
20km alongside the park fence flat with Defence
Force bodies. This was no Guns of Navarone at
Eyethu Cinema, double attraction, with Kelly's
Heroes, midnight show. No applause or catcalls,
no whistlings & excited shouts of 'sterring',
'ntwana'... No. It was betrayal from the top that
brought it. The National Hero had sold them out,
we heard later.

But there was still the last firefight... for hours
the soldiers circled above, and crept in the
undergrowth. There was much fear in their
ranks. & they bled. & died. What they had been

taught was a lie, they realised. As many & more
flopped down, their chests blown up, heads
smashed, legs twisted under them. & the glaze
settling over the eyes. & still more came. A white
army against three young black men. & the sun
beat down, coward yellow like gaseous pus. It
couldn't hold forever. Toppled down from the
apex. Leaned over, like holding its stomach to
keep intestines in. 'Let them not touch the ground
or it is over.' Ulibambe lingashoni. Hold it up,
the sun, or it sets with you. & when it went down
they followed it down too. They died with it.

After the switch-over, in the new dispensation's
stinky after-birth, they, the ones with power,
went to dig up the Sasol Three and 'bring them
home'. They held a commemoration service at the
amphitheatre in the township. And thousands
came, and sang praises. & the traitor National
Hero made a speech. Talking about honour in
life and heroism in death. & the people clapped.
& some cried, touched. There was much in the
air that was ugly at core, even though glistening
golden on the outside. & all went home. & the
three remained in the new ground.

(dog turds cooked in vomit. & served with piss
gravy.
I appreciate your racial generosity on my plate.
Deep stomach filling. I feel it in my lining like

history's lint.)

Vegetative state above surface & below the manure
forms promise feeding 'resurrection'?
Pull the plug. Rather a poem breeding inspiration.

> STORM – WORM
> POEM – FORM

I am content
Revolting within makes me content out
Revolt in here thrusts trust out there
'crowd a people vote for me'

'A heart that isn't tainted – no greater breastplate!' a street preacher screams into the night.

Maletsholo's daughter slipped, slid off the silver pipe across the Klip River and drowned. Running there i found a crowd gathered, whispering about how it was a sign someone was bound for traditional healership in the family. Children don't just go under the water unless they are called by the ancestors. & also, why would the child have tried crossing the river over this sewer-pipe when the road was a short distance away? They had seen her, some say, like a trapeze

artist on the shiny pipe, one foot snaking after
the other. Agile. No safety care. & then she'd slid
down, slow, they say, unlike one who'd tripped.
She'd grasped helplessly, for some hold, but the
pipe was slippery. & so down she'd gone. No
need for tears though, they said to the mother.
The world beyond had called, the little girl
had answered. & you'd see, in no time one in
the family would be called for initiation to the
sangoma realm.

Maletsholo's my aunt. & when my cousin Dinky
walked in on a snake in the kitchen and killed
it with a ladle, that was a sign. Since she'd had
a fortnight of nightmares, waking up screaming
some nights, singing in her sleep others, they
took her off to the spirit medium and there she
stayed for a year. Came back a healer. But first,
on this day, Maletsholo's sister who worked at
Matlhapa's Funeral Undertakers, where the little
girl was taken after being fished out of Kliprivier
– Maletsholo's sister, who once said she'd cooled
her alcohol on the dead bodies, came staggering
drunk into the house. She stumbled in and said:
'Oh my sister, look at the tears on my face, i
am touched, no i am not crying. Today i washed
your daughter, her carcass i mean... and oh, you
don't know how beautiful she looked, yessis, i
have never seen such beauty on a person dead
or alive... it is clear the water-snake licked her

face all the time she was down there, it removed
all the blemishes and she came out beautiful,
oh you don't know how lucky you are, such a
gorgeous corpse... i am so jealous, she looked just
so lovely...'

& Maletsholo toppled down. Collapsed. Out.

I walk into the tavern and greet. Everyone. Walk
to the toilet and it's flooded. I stand before the
urinal filthy liquid climbing up my shoes, socks
getting wet. Drip off walk out and outside the
door this man, older than me, is standing there.
Look of fury. He says: 'Yeah, you greeted me,
hm, for what? Tell me why, to do what?' Ugly
grimace under the sweat and the fat on the face.
Unwashed, the water runs black down the cheeks.
Like a stun-gun going off, the words. Shock of it
sends the electricity hitting my system and i reel.
Coiling up. It moves in jerky flows, i move off
before the white light comes. He wouldn't be able
to stand up afterwards. I see, in my head, that
swarthy face split open and the life-fluid spill out.

I hit the pavement soft in my tread, walk into
a riot. Service undelivered. No water. No trash
picked up. The filth, paper packaging, food left
over, dog turds, insanely all over. The mass is out.
Overturning dustbins. They fill the street. Noise.
Some old women, hawkers, sit on blankets on
the pavement. Their wares before them. Second-
hand clothing. Some traditional medication, herbs
and little bushes, dried. Vegetables laid out on
newspapers. There, fruits shined, on upturned
cardboard boxes. The crowd comes on, kick the
stuff over, spill bottles. It is black Christmas on

the street-side. They throw cabbages & potatoes into the street, out to the gutters. They squelch tomatoes, grab bananas, apples, pears and munch away, not angry now, just laughing. They dig in and take as they please. There is singing. Some dancing. The sellers, the old women, they protest in silence. Object in scared wordlessness. The quietness damming the rage within, the helpless anger and the bile of disgust rising behind their chapped lips. The rioters pick still, choose some, trickle off. I look at the old women trembling under the shawls over their shoulders, shaking drooping heads. & i know something has turned here, some tide. Their children will surely not eat tonight, the looters ate on their behalf. Though mud, when it dries, tastes like chocolate, they say here.

'Their badges serve no purpose. They rush out when the least threatening things happen. I don't know why they call them police. Look, OK, if you slap your woman and she goes there, you will see how many vans will come for you, with those stupid sirens going like bleeding jackals, and the blue lights flashing... but what happened when the filling station was hit, hm? These guys who work there, they were locked in the storeroom at the back. The robbers said you keep your heads down. If you just lift your eyes that is the end of you. We will tell you when you can stand up: right

now, stay there on your stomachs, on the floor.
Where is the money? Quick...

'They took the money and locked them in there,
the arm of each one chained to the steel bench.
The next thing, there was a great noise like the
earth was getting cut deep, it shook so hard
the glass windows broke and the filling station
attendants thought they were dying. & the time
was not even ten, the night was thin... still, we
heard the sound in the township, a kilometre
away. So why did the police station not hear it
if we could, is it also not in the township? Why
were the police deaf? The robbers bombed the
ATM... in the morning there were bits of paper
money all torn up and ink everywhere but i tell
you, the police were nowhere... But have some
trouble in your house with your people and see...
cowards, i tell you.' He shook his head, his arm
rising to his face, leaned back against the bottle-
store wall, and took a swig on his quart of Black
Label. I grabbed my plastic bag with my six pack,
notebook, pen and cigarette box in it, bade him
a dry bye and went off down the road, in the
direction of the Indian shop.

A small van drove slowly past me, edging close
to the shop storefront. A few metres away a little
boy in a torn vest and dirty shorts stood looking
at the approaching van, inside it two ruddy-faced,

senior citizen white women. Just when the van drew abreast of him the child broke into a grin, grabbed his crotch and shouted: 'fuckie fuckie, missis... hehehe' at the van and ran off, shrieking, into the undergrowth. The women drove on up to the shop and parked. It started to drizzle. I ran to get under the cover of the store's roof. On the stoep stood a group of teenaged boys, striking rather odd poses, like they were modelling. The women, who were old, did not get out of the van. I walked on and put my back against the shop wall, reaching for a cigarette. There was debate inside the van. The boys stood, silently, looking at them. Words exchanged inside the vehicle, shaken heads, disagreement. The one woman, seemingly in charge, was pointing from one boy to the other, going down the line. Saying something to her mate, who was hesitant, from my distance, shaking her head each time, until, at last, consensus, it looked like... the one window got opened, on the side of the commander, who stuck her head out and said: 'Jy met die wit hemp, kom'... The white-shirted boy pointed a finger at himself, 'Ek?' 'Ja.'

He cast a quick look at his friends, disentangled himself, and sauntered over to the van. He leaned into the open window. Negotiations in the skin trade. The commander was pleased, smiled. Her friend seemed embarrassed, looked furtively around, as if to check if anyone was watching as the boy nodded. Looked over at his friends, gestured, finger of one hand pointed at the wrist of the other, saying 'ka di nako, later', and climbed into the back seat. And the car coughed to life, reversed, inched away. A high-pitched voice behind me said 'hm, ba ile go mo ja' – they are going to eat him. I turned quickly around as a thick, middle-aged woman hastened into the shop. I stand there. Head empty. And the rain falls slow. The place clears.

*

*So Dave Brubeck White playing at some campus
they wouldn't let him bring his bassist within
sight of the applause & put him behind the
curtain. Disembodied bass-lines. Then what
happened? Halfway through he got to: 'hey man,
you are playing too far back come out front' & they
crashed, killed, destroyed the place. So now the
consciously Black hates... come on, man...*

*YOU ARE SO BLACK you shouldn't be on
SLAVOJ ZIZEK'S lap...
riding his dick so hard every time you open your
snout
out spurts eastern European semen... mixed, of
course, with your crap...
& you stand there, tongue out, ready to lap it up!...
take time out!
(don't be dead & brave putting it on Dave.
Go down Mississippi river running down the
legacy of the slave.
Marooned, northern starred out, Unmastered.
Comes the cat from Hades
getting the Congo Squared down to Roots.
Making rattles out of broken ankles. Yes, plus the
shattered shackles.
Now with convenience stored up & forgotten,
sounds had to choose: record or jail-bars.
There we have it, the music comes bearing scars.*

MAMOTABI'S HOUSE – White City was Black Slum.

2 rooms then 3. Ezindlovini. The place of elephants. It could be storming out but inside would be like the inside of an elephant... POTELA's knife cutting through the air at my mother and MAKHULU grabbing it mid-flight... she still bears the scars. Smoke in the night. Lost consciousness. Came to, outside in the air, being fanned.

My grandmother's hands were PARCHMENT. Deep lined. I read them. They were my first script. House of hospitality. & great violence. & so its character constantly changed. Fluxed.

Vincent lived there. & brought me first face up with the politics of my reality. Joe Mahlangu with the croaking laugh. It started and stayed in his stomach. At night he'd go out and shoot people coupling.

I grew up between a guerrilla and a serial killer. If i didn't write i could have been either one.

BUNIONS ON MY FINGERS... I PUT IN A LOT OF WORK ON THE PEN.
Left blood on pages. Mine and mosquitoes'.
Metal tip on paper screech... night-time

soundtrack.
Closer deeper than the shebeen's when
i double-tongue my thoughts. Channel emotion.

'No melody to remember/ no beat to dance to'.
Armstrong came on, a dong creeping on be-bop
arse. He went away dizzied & urethra parkered
up so much his pop-eyes stayed on stalks so long
they couldn't close his coffin... down the hip hop
decades.

Caught in the rhythm-current pull... harmonic
scrum... Beat-wave swept over... went down
under... in the tug & pull... got choked in the
melodics... no CPR, they wouldn't... he had vomit
all over his mouth from air-blowing trumpets.

Sonar-Versification from here to Prose-Silence.

The knob flickered red on the TECHNICS 1210
MK11 & the arm dropped, the stylus got the wax
ahiss: 'titsotsi ta Joni ti ni hlamarisile'. Johannes
Mangwele on the turntable was ripping guts. The
electrified intestines taut, brittle & deadly. No
licks these. Cyclical travel into the multi-versified.
Out to the sonarsphere.

Good morning blue lights, how do you do,
bureaucRAT?
The coppers, they rubber-stop arse...
sodomised with a baton at the police station.
The station commander was found later

licking the chocolate off the baton-head.

Death in the mouth. & a sanguine anus.
Bleeding ulcers in excretion. Chamber-pot
orchestra.
Dental infections inflect these words. Verbal
cirrhosis.

The touching, the heat, the wetness. The throb &
pulse of this... Our Thing.
& lying there, watching you sleep. The beauty of
this being. I feel deep wretchedness. Filths me
down. & i sink. Into the septic tank of... my self.
It flays me, rubs the skin off my bones. I feel like
a psychopath. Killing you each day, over and over.

The veins shut down. At the point of bursting.
Eaten up & out by my inability to love you.

Dizzy Gillespie: 'When i first met Charlie Parker, it was similar to a laser. He impressed me more than anybody to that point. Charlie Parker had a new approach to playing music, we had the music... but we didn't have the... should i say, pyrotechnics...'

Cyclical. As black music. Inching towards The Invocation. Calling up the spirits. They need the beat over and over, falling in 'same time'... might be polyrhythmic but has to LAND on the same... BEAT. Write that!

This place is called SEDING, short for 'Leseding', place of light. Quite ironic given the darkness throbbing at its core and spilling out bubbling in the blackest rage when least expected.

Surrounded by farmland in all directions, it is a settlement of about 700 households crammed in tiny structures. Average 7 souls per hovel. It used to be made up of ramshackle, corrugated iron shacks that seemed tossed down regardless of aesthetics. Then the new administration's housing programme kicked in.

Smell of cowdung of invisible cattle mixed with petrol gets you lifted, 6am filling station. Only

place open for cigarettes. And you realise 'we
can't go back to the bheshu and umkhonto'.

The Marico River 10 minutes walk away, and
no Jol'iinkomo in the air. The maidens walk by
dressed in blue overalls. The municipality's had
another call open for 'conservation'. They are
signed up to kill the alien plants growing along
the river, more than 200km. The plants, they
drain the water. And non-indigenous, must go.
And they line their Black experience up. For less
than minimal pay.

They call it Heritage Day. When beef gets
braaied, nationally. Throws that history into
assegai-sharpened-on-not-so-old-bones relief. I
have Nongqawuza mornings, watching frock-
decked smoke in tiekiedraai twirl rise over the
Dwarsberg, and wonder...

At the Culture Centre at festival time Afrikaners
bring out the dozen black teens, in loincloths and
carting drums, plus an assortment of percussion
instruments, to sin-tertain the touristy gawkers.

Weekends it is Bikers' Paradise. Early dawn the
roar of powerful motorbikes spreads itself across
the bush and bounces off the mountains on either
side. And they come. On their human-hunts.

'I took a... i don't know... a big beer bottle... i was gonna crown this guy.' – Dizzy Gillespie

'I felt that... ehm... one had to take Heroin to play like Charlie Parker played... / by doing the very thing that killed... THE WAY WE CELEBRATED Bird's passing was to go out and use some junk.' – Frank Morgan

*

Max Roach. Give me no temptation towards diss-infestation. Spraying beats like napalm... crash-test dum-dum healing effect, though. The churched-up symbolism. After the listen... the ghosts came in person.
Blessed spirit reign from land of Ogun to the American.

Leave Segwagwa to crack-walk his hands on those meropa, wrapped in animal skin. Yes, Yakhal'inkomo for those drums to be. Sacrifice, badimo demanded. Leave Thobejane alone, drop the comparison like Shasha's drumstrick breaking the snare's back, then brush-caress the tom, cat!

Albert... Ailer? Ah, Ayler, yeah, that's deep sickness.

Hawk ins-&-outs, Coleman. They come to feed, the predator-birds. Blood spurt out the snout spangle-fanged.

Super/ sub doesn't matter stand & salute or go out!

BUSHVELD DAYS — caught between the abusive forlorn thieves & police crooks —

Early mornings i sit on the kitchen stoep with coffee and cigarettes, and a pair of birds, without fail, come and perch on the telephone line opposite and sing to me. They wear the Botswana flag. Blue, black and white. They nest in the massive tree just behind the wires, there is a hole dug into the bark. I often hear little chirps and squeaks from in there. Their babies.

And then there is the squirrel family. They come running a few metres past me, days. I do not know what happened that day, but as mister squirrel dashed past, the one bird swooped and klapped squirrel on the back, hard. Squirrel let out a yell and scampered. A few hours later the squirrel eased its way close, closer even, to where i was sitting. Until it was a metre away. Stood on its hind legs and rubbed its paws, its mouth opening and closing. I told it i understood, it was telling what the turmoil had been about, what led to the fallout with the bird. It stood looking at me for a while, lowered its paws to the ground, and went off.

PIET MAMPOER... well, he distils mampoer on his farm. The police shut him down. Tourists kept falling sick. Their innards burning, being carted off to the hospital 42km away. His stuff was poison, it was said. More than 80% pure. The black people run off the road in panic when he drives down. He can kill you, that one, they say. He has killed a few. Make sure to not be on the road at night when he comes down. He could drive you down, smash you to tiny pieces, gather them up and bury you on the farm, to make the fruit trees grow better.

Bottles broken and eyes empty of life, withered dreamy sights. Despair town place of purgatory. Whose and what sins are these walking down past ghostly ancient walled & haunted window-eyes of shops that haven't been open in a decade... and the urine marks trail down the dry twiggy legs of mothers and children alike. Emaciated, same as the mongrels sniff-snuff... and mucus dried up with the last rains. In the bush-sun, the heat clogs the pores. Hits the top of the skull and the pain shoots down to the centre of the feet.

She went to report the rape. And the policemen on night duty, the two... gawked, drooled, looking at her torn clothes, the thighs showing. And took her into the station commander's office. There was no one there. And AGAIN the womb screamed against the raping sperm.

The township could take up a quarter of Wagter's farm. He says 'I bought this place for R20 000 in '92, just before the changes. It goes right down to the river...' Wagter is an artist, a painter and sculptor. He was commissioned by the 'democratic structures' to make a sculpture of Sol Plaatje in Kimberley. He made the Plaatje figure seated at a desk, pen in hand. But the councillor of Kimberley, fresh from a trip to Cuba, came, saw the artwork and said no, she had seen the sculptures of revolutionaries in Havana, they were twice the size of a tall man, and were proud warrior depictions. Plaatje should abandon the desk, stand up and wave his black fist in the air.

Pauline says her property is even bigger. Yes this side it also goes to the river. But it crosses the street this side and goes right up to the mountain. 'In '92 Fantasma called me, she couldn't breathe she so was excited... she said, "Come quickly, don't ask questions. Come... and don't forget your cheque-book." I left my parents' farm in the Free State and came. And here i stayed.'

POGISHO works at the bottle store. He says: 'I
have worked for this beetroot-coloured pig-faced
guy since i was a little boy, when i should have
been at school. Oh i loved my father and mother,
bless them. I would have been dressing in a suit
and sitting in an office otherwise, i would have
gone to college, but they died and i came and
worked for this fat fuck. I am nearly 40 now. He
pays me R400 per week. 400! And you know what,
let us say on Saturday he will give me R100, on
Tuesday another R50 and so on until it is R400.
No, fuck this. I am not working today. I sat there
earlier today with my head between my knees,
just sitting, not working. His daughter brought
me a plate of food and i took it and tossed it on
the ground. I am sick of these people. He came
and found me still sitting and said: 'Is jy gesuip?'
I just sat there for a while. Then he asked me:
'Aha, het jy weer twak-tabak gerook?' I said:
'Meneer, jy is nie my pa nie, my pa het my nie
eens daai ding gevra nie...' I was waiting for him
to try his baasskap on me, i was going to hit him
in his pig-face so hard...

'Look, i know everything in this place, prices and
all, the stock, everything. I have spent my life
here but when he and his wife cannot run the
place, like he drinks a lot, you can see by his face,

and he conks out sometimes. And his wife falls
ill to death a few times but they will never let
me run the place or sit behind the cash-machine,
they go and get some Afrikaner person who
cannot even count or use the machines here and
has to ask me... what is that? Like because i am
black, i will steal? No, i am going to bleksem him
moertoe! My wife worked here too, you know that,
for some years. She has got a terrible ailment.
Her belly-button started swelling up badly, ah
it is bad, and what happened? They just threw
her aside, not a cent, nothing, to hell with them!
He thinks he knows me, okay i will show him
something he doesn't know...'

"Dear Anna-Tommy-Carly... this writing thing
is cramming my head. & it is progressive
over-population. Good i can still call it back,
exhale, let out, watch it blow up & away, fizzle
out & down, flop out of breath, weak & beat
settle. BUT 'til when the soft landing, or even
take off? What when i can no longer channel,
reign, sin rule my kinkdom? Control this cunt-
tree of my skunk... i mean skull... prune, cut
it down or even burn down to the ash-blue-
ball congested ground-nuts? The writer is in
an unsynthetised fix. The literary critic puts
his pipe in his navy-coloured-lipped mouth,
strikes a match with much practiced flare, his
one hand, the one off the matchstick, loosens

his collar, sucks deep, blows a hornless rhino smoke-ring & says in all honest hoarseness: 'All texts are pre-existent. Maybe just not manifest. Forget the original impulse.' Just write true to the formula & the SA literary awards cabal will give you an award..."

The brandy is quite strong tonight, though the same brand as last week's. Emotion adds much alcohol-content to that specified on the bottle. & from the corner my Hendrixian hero, the greatest living session guitarist to ever walk the blue planet, his own idol notwithstanding, a sad, ultra-sensitive individual whose own compositions i find quite bloodless & too diabetes-factored, lets his electric-guitar toned voice solo: 'It's just like children, fear of the dark. Baseless. Better the born raceless.' My ultimate rhymester sinks back onto the pillow he has been sitting on. & it is a quiet moment like when the applause dies down & there is no encore. & nobody knows what the script, or the tracklisting demands. So my hero grabs his guitar. He'd been boring the gathered, endlessly tuning. The strings pulling at veins. Strums some hesitant chords, kills Jimi with the first bar, looks at no one, & lets the lyrics i wrote for him float out. His singing voice walks on clogs, graceless. But the twinkly fingers on the wood carry... & it is silent to the last sub-throaty note in this room, pyrotechnical magic-fingered guitar-licking in the pauses.

★

Sibelius Scandinavian jingoistic...

Work on. Dyani-bass-powered. African man Zim Nqgawana more melodic Sankara than Varara. Cohen's democracy coming to the US like that Yeatsian beast to Bethlehem.

Nation time Baraka without the anti-Semite. Root of his chameleon-ideology nibbling away, termites. Zion is a cock though in Hebrew. 'Gal, run come climb holy mount Zion', dance-hall jam. Salvation at the dry end of ejaculate. Flip the immaculate onto her arse. See the hypocrite skanking to Tosh militant recruiting black soldiers...

This little Afrikaner boy, must be 16 or so, has just greeted me with the utmost respect: 'Môre, oupa!' Shit can't get stinkier than that. Oh foxsakes. Reminds me of the child in the shop in the Free State, who said to Raks while rubbing his hands together in all humility: 'Askies, Oom Kaffir, kan u asseblief vir my lekkergoed koop?'

All these spin around as i scribble, in the garden of the shebeen, with the one section partitioned off behind a bamboo-wall & i sit there, with beer & small bodied Pogisho, who says he weighs 58kg, & his wife, Mmaphefo, who is 105kg, with a

pair of quart bottles & they talk while i listen, in-
between jotting down a little scribbling along my
way this Sunday morning.

Thanya Sepoti, the shebeen/ tavern, used to be
called Tanya's Spot until the natives twisted that
around when the Afrikaner owners gave up in the
face of belligerent native drunkenness and sold it
to these Chinese immigrants. It is the nucleus of
all black activity here.

Pogisho & Mmaphefo, couple, work the graveyard
tavern shift. Mixing with the bones & flayed flesh.
She is huge, both front and back, that is, a huge
paunch that hangs half-way down her thighs,
and a posterior that follows far behind when she
walks. She is tall too. And extends some distance
sideways. He is a slip of a man, tiny. Small. He
reaches hardly to her shoulder, standing up. It is
said all those disparities fall away when people
lie down. It must be a mouse-on-a-bread-loaf
situation with them. They are loving to each
other. Right now they are close to crying, saying
while their voices entwine so much i cannot tell
who is saying what:

'You know, we have a 13-year-old son. &
last year, when the year was getting split &
everybody was eating drinking having fun, we
have these 'scales', you know, the jam-tins, full

of Jija, Sekgonyamatlho, we could not afford
beer because, well, hey thank the gods for this
Chinese guy here, you know him he owned the
shop on the corner & the people chased him away
but before he left, just as Christmas coming, he
gave us things from his shop & our child got a
shirt, & fine pants &... ok, it was only the shoes
that spoilt things but he looked beautiful like all
the other children. The reason, look at it, i have
worked there for 19 years, both of us... you found
me there, Pogisho, didn't you? You have been here
what, 17? Anyway, when i fell ill the white people
here did not know me, they would not even let
me get into their bottle store. Look, for the first
five years i earned R250. OK, those were the days
things were not expensive like today. Oh, after
two years it became R300. In another year R400...
oh, per week... yes. After all that time i was
earning R400 per week... & every time i have to
negotiate again for my money that he promised...
you know i had to go to the woman to get a pay-
slip for... something... i think a tax document. &
the husband wrote it out on a piece of paper &
put R1000 per week there. & i said but i don't get
paid this. He said no, tell them you get paid that.
& it is a piece-job you are working, not full-time.
Hm, he must think i am a child. Anyway, you
have not seen me for a while because i said, no,
fuck this... after last week i went to him for pay
& he gave me R60 for the week, saying he will

see me next week. & then his daughter asked me
to wash her car & gave me R30. That is terrible.
I have to always beg for my pay. After all these
years...

'& now my son, he is 13. What a beautiful boy,
he looks like a girl &... you know, that kid will
never, when i want to give him pocket-money,
accept it. No, he will say, Pogisho, do you have
smokes? & if i say no, he will say no, just let me
have R1 & you buy something to smoke with the
rest... & now he made me sad, came home & said
this boer wants them to go pick the weeds out of
his farm &... he will give them each R10. I nearly
cried because i know my child will go there, get
beaten up & sworn at, & then later after the day
in the burning sun get paid R10 &... he will bring
it home to his mother, he will not even take a
cent... & my tv is dead, i bought him this game
with the control you play on the tv screen, so
he can't play & i cannot fix it... i want to please
my child too, like other parents... but when the
tv is fine & i watch it & i see all those children
twisting their mouths at their parents & giving
them these heavy-ball voices & demanding this
& this in their huge houses with all the white
values i think what a lucky man i am... & my
wife... anyway on new year's day a young guy
came & saw us drinking this Jija thing and said
no, we were making him sad, so he bought us a

case of Black Label, hm... blessed... how do you like that?'

One night 2 am. R1 500 counted & in the moneybag. More in the till. The last of the customers trickling out... He needs to go to the toilet outside. She is uneasy. Premonition. She tells him: urinate inside, behind the beer-crates. He says no, they work there, they will suffer the stench. He goes out the back, just around the building's corner, pulls out, splashes, one eye on the front-door. Sees two men watching him from directly opposite the door with the steel grating. They move towards him, he does not trust them, so he nips his piss & moves towards the back door. His left forearm is in Plaster of Paris. They grab him as he opens the grille. Struggle ensues. One guy hits his hand with an object he doesn't see. He staggers back, tries to fight. They push him in. After cracking his lip.

Meanwhile, on the other side, through the front door, a man comes in, orders a single loose cigarette. He is short 30 cents. They empathise. Hand it to him. From behind the bird-coop cage. Little hole cut through to fit just one hand or the passing of a beer-bottle. The knifings. She pisses where she stands. The urine-smoke rises from the spot directly between her legs. Her 'in-betweens' she calls the area between one leg and another.

Pogisho slides through after she has hit the man
at the front right in the middle of his head with
the steel-centred wood-covered cue-stick and he
reels back, dazed. & Pogisho splits the one guy's
lip open with the Plaster-of-Paris'd arm. He
slides croc-like, all fours, fast & smooth through
the urine surrounding her frame & still dripping
down from her vagina. He slides in and hits his
head against the opposite wall inside the chicken-
coop-like enclosure & she slams the grille shut.
They decide to wash the blood out of their mouths
with Carling Black Label. Man & woman. Each
with their own quart. They gurgle & swallow,
blood & alcohol, & their bond is sealed further.
Arms around each other as the hours pass on,
slow, towards daylight.

BAAS calls at 4 am, gets the news, he calls the
police station. The fat policemen, two policeman
and two policewomen arrive, swearing. Hurling
insults at her, saying she is a known drunkard.
'What is this shit all about? It is that drunkard
woman!'

'Hey, why did we get out of the police-station? Do
you know how busy we are?'

'We have no time for your poison-guzzling
weepiness &... shoo, you stink!'

'Where are the robbers?' the policewoman asks,
as if they expected her to hold them there while
waiting for the cops. They are full of disdain.
Badge-powered, & made manly by uniform & gun
on child-bearing hip. They hobble away. Leave
the stench of their office to follow after them. Not
a cent was taken.

Dawn breaks. Baas comes in, checks the money,
turns around and says he is missing money for 3
beer cases. Mmaphefo weeps, heavily, pulling it
all from her guts. Missus arrives. Accounts are
tallied. R15 000 in the money-bag, R3 000 in the
till. Blood and piss all over. She thanks Pogisho
and Mmaphefo, still bleeding where they were cut
up, with R300. Mmaphefo lets the tears roll at
the cheap price of their Black lives. & still, their
13-year-old child will grow. Their son. Despite it
all. If that crowded graveyard across the dustway
doesn't call.

*I've heard stories. They dug a shallow hole and
put a metal sheet on top & left it. Maybe the rain
would come & make music. Perhaps it would bake
in there like the ancients. Both the hard hit &
the soft massage put you to sleep. I feel like with
Fusion they brought syrup. Sewers went open
hand & the drumstick is the brush so as not to
push the drums central, some kind of caress or
anaesthetic.*

How you sound Baraka?

Black F/Art... you decide Pa-Ra-Pa-Rap

*Horns & Drums kicking in is quite narcotic.
'Wailers are we...' Pa-Ra-Pa-Rap. Black Dada
inching closer to wreck. Dud. I heard Eliot read &
it was... inching deeper inside my car. Nihilismus,
despite the hate, rage... was so white, just dressed
in blackskin. Anti-Semite.*

Termite at the houtkop, even.

*I wished for Black Noise crash like under a
psychopathic smith's hammer off rhythm*

*Fist to fist became knives, axes, machetes then
cowardice graduated that to guns then the safety
of cowardice hit you from long way come the
Bomb-masters & now... from the comfort of the
lounge in here, meet the Drone.*

The sister of the shebeen queen joins us & i
try to get a recipe for fried cabbage, like my
grandmother used to make. She is 24, holding
the fort while the owner is off to church, she says,
says some customer who has just gone into the
house was stinky & she hates being here, can't
wait to be away. She is caramel pretty-faced &
wearing thick make-up & long fake eyelashes,

eyebrows cut to razor-edge. Her belly hangs over her jeans. Her legs thin, though. The whole impression incongruous. & she says she is not of this place. Just visiting her sister 'with the Chinese child'. Soon gone. She cradles a glass which she says contains Coca-Cola & offers it to Mmaphefo so she 'can take some of the edge off the alcohol'.

She is taking extra-studies for her matric & she knows my son has gone through university in Joburg, could he come help her with her mathematics? & no, he will be perfectly safe but as i know, everyone gets tempted. & if there is temptation & he does not rape & there is agreement between them then why should i worry? She speaks over everyone else & others argue ingredients & cooking-mode so she rips my pen & notebook out of my hand & writes, telling me there is no better way... then giving it back with a huge, satisfied smile. I open to the page & read:

Instruction of cooking cabbage
Cutting onion + green paper + carrotts and frying it, with oil
After that you put cabbage in pot,
Containing it with, carrotts, green paper + together with salt.
And Raja medium.

At this point she, Mmaphefo & her husband start arguing between them. Someone says seasoning after the pot has started boiling or cooking is a bad idea because when i eat, like say if it is a chicken dish, the meat itself will be tasteless, in this case the cabbage, but all the flavour will be in the gravy, don't i know that? Anyway, before cooking the cabbage i should wash it & set it aside for the water to get drained out.

& someone says no potato, it puts water in the pot. & another says hell no, cabbage & potato same time. To boil. & salt too.

& i write in my book:
Not a HOWL (that's massa's, jackal caught in my t/rap
Mine is a field-holler... Your dollar's not worth
My dog-collar...

I go off to try cook my 'churchical' screaming cabbage.

NO NO NO. My AWB neighbour is getting rather familiar these days. Calling my number under silly pretexts. Tonight saying she has no water and 'do i have some?'... fok... why am i watering right-wing-shit?... I hope she hasn't searched out 'black power' online and seen how the smut-people have perverted it and now, perhaps, i have become desirable... 'oh lawd have mercy'. Her husband ran off with a black woman, let us not forget.

THE SHAMAN came here and worked as a gardener tending the church-grounds. In time he ran off with the predikant's wife. But not much of a distance, though. They live a two minute walk away from the NG Kerk where he used to work and she to 'wife'. Now he does nothing with his days but sit on the stoep welcoming visitors and keeping this one room in the house where women are not allowed to enter. People believe he has something supernatural about him. Wagter says he walked with him in the Kgalagadi and at odd points he could not see him even though he was by his side. He would be present but just not there, in a corporeal sense.

The shaman is extremely thin, frail, fragile. He loves hugs. And when you embrace him you can feel his spine protruding from his back through his clothes. It is hard to imagine him having sex with her. She is extremely strong and energetic. A pure-breed of an Afrikaner vrou but... she loves him lots, you can see it when she looks at him. Something you cannot point at passes over her face. Other men around here fear having him around their wives. They sneak in close and check the extent and quality of the hug when their wives move in for their fair share. He just needs to hug people. That is just how he is. I have decided to have no gardener in my yard for as long as i still can handle a sickle. I never do, though. I offer others a little money and watch them work. I have put a no-hugging law in place in my home. I am wary.

I bring a complaint about the crap conduct of a couple of cops, to the police station commander, a black woman. She listens, eyes wide, then does the Pontius Pilate, saying the matter is 'above' her, she will have to consult her superior, a white Afrikaans male working in a police station in a different town altogether. This is rather sad, calling on Makhulu-baas, or what? I don't know. I thought she was boss there, refers to her officers as her 'children', so... hm... i wait for the 'feedback' she promised.

Parked at the intersection of the N4, a couple stand next to the car, on the pavement. Waiting for traffic to pass before driving across. A police van comes and stops, edge of the inner lane, waiting for a truck coming in the opposite direction to pass so the police van can turn. The driver glances across at our car, sees us, eyes grow wild, he turns looking at us. What is going on?

At the Municipality Office, a staff of ten crowds in there, it is attached to the tiny library. They loll around all day, exchanging gossip. Never been known to do any work. Now and then someone will come in wanting a photocopy. R3 for a page. If coming off the printer (there are a couple of computers for public use) each page costs R1. I never got the logic.

They flap tongues in there, the workers:

'What use is a man if he does not buy you things'....'Oh, that poor man walking down the street, you know that is not his child that woman claims is, no, she gave pussy up to the neighbour'... 'How do you know?'... 'Everybody knows.'

The police station is one street down. Unlike city ones anybody can just walk in and up to the charge office. None of those security bars and turnstiles one finds in Joburg or Soweto where the police have to barricade themselves against potential attack.

The post office is on the same street. The same post office i went to get my post sent by overnight mail and the two women, the teller and the cleaner burst out laughing, hugging their sides when i enquired. They thought it a world class

joke and told me to come back after two days.
'Who has ever heard of mail posted yesterday and
you come just the next day to collect it? Where is
this man from hahaha...'

I have never seen anybody except the Afrikaners
walk with any purpose here. Snail life.
Everything is slowed down to drug-induced pace,
like. You cannot see the slime trails. The drool off
faces you can, though.

I have heard 'nnywana gago' and 'marete a rrago'
from the mouths of children and adults here more
than anywhere else. Foul mouths are plentiful
here. The expression is coarse. Parallels the
existence. People swear, it is written into the
relations. Sex is on the level of the shop-counter.

*

*Montgomery? Tabane's worse in the killing-fields.
Strum or pluck like a bomb hit electric-storm
struck. Guitar-strings wrapped around your
soul. Lilt or growl & anything in between when
the strangulation need comes so you have to pick
nearer the neck than... k/not! & then shovel the
dissonant shit out like the musical night-soil-man
leaning the chamber-pot against the door so in
the morning when you open for some fresh air the
dead stench, faeces & piss spills in. Take that, you
tone-deaf!*

TAKALANI, first time i saw him i thought him
a psychopath, someone no woman or child would
be safe around. The man is huge, tall, looks
retarded (gets off on showing people gory pictures
in magazines, scenes of torture, innards showing,
mutilation, while cackling like a hyena, looking at
the horror, or disgust in whoever he is displaying
it to...). First time i saw him, even before the
pictures, i thought him capable of slitting your
throat and feeding off your liver, or lungs, or...
and drinking your blood to wash your brains
down.

Takalani is in charge of the water services. And
also runs the little library attached. He is good
with children, Takalani, they crowd around him

and he reads stories to them. Gives them quizzes to help them with their schoolwork.

On Friday Takalani listens to a query about the filth in the water. And says 'Yeah well, it is Friday, i am closing the office. What, it is two hours too early? So what, i want to go and drink now, at the shebeen, my weekend is starting. The water is brown, true... but what can i do? We do not have the chemicals to clean it. We will see about it next week.'

One street down, at the clinic, next to the police station, the queues lengthen, children howling pitifully, clutching their bellies. & the adults look on, keeping it in. Running stomachs in here. & the cemetery a block up keeps eating up new ground, inching closer to the township. & the houses look on, eyes wide, as the jungle of death-mounds creeps closer still, like the jungle beyond. Look on the positive side of it, the BLACKS ARE OCCUPYING LAND IN DEATH they cannot in life. EACH DAY MORE SPACE TAKEN, 'izwe lethu!' The land is ours their forebears screamed under white rule, but they do not scream for it anymore. They die to take it back.

In the Indian shop this drunken almost-to-crawling woman looks at me and says: 'Oooh, i like this brother with the old fashioned beret... I am going home with you, lovey...' I run off without what i went in there for.

I need to work on my dress code. My grooming too, i think. I really hope i can, by some stretch of the imagination, be called a 'writer' and we know how those are supposed to be poor. But that is still no excuse for this drunken farmer in a van to drive up and offer me a bunch of 20c coins... and he looked so sad when i refused... baas-turd business, this.

SPENCER works at the Indian shop. Works for the guy who short-changes the old and the illiterate. And when forced to give change he hands sweets over. Spencer tells me what not to buy at the shop, and points out foodstuff that is past its expiry date but still sits on the shelf for the unvigilant. Spencer put the Chinese-man who ran Thanya Sepoti shebeen onto this young woman from a deep place some distance away. He played match-maker. And ducked a knife from her boyfriend. Spencer made off with her, with the Chinese guy, fresh to the land, huffing by his side. She moved in. Off to the side of the shebeen there is a three-room structure used for residential purposes. She moved in and now there is a baby afro-chinese running around.

Anyway, the shebeen got off running, packed

month-end and weekends. The money piled up.
& then Spencer moved in. And the Chinese guy
(along with his numerous brothers) moved out,
never to be seen again. Her sister got called over,
roped in. And now Spencer does it to both of them.
On the sly. I saw him stumble out of the shebeen
at dawn. I asked if he was now The Priest. He
said well, he couldn't just keep going to church all
his life. Yes, now he is the one who holds services
and gives sermons and benedictions. The shebeen
is a place of worship, see? For Spencer the whole
deal had been a business plan and now he was
raking in the profits.

SETUMO has a scar running right across his
throat from when someone tried to off him. His
voice seems to cut from some place other than his
mouth. A weird ventriloquist act. He is a good
guy, works for the justice department. Advised
me once to report the police to the Independent
Police Investigation Directorate, for their
intimidation and extortion tactics, he offered to
drive me there. On this day, though, he stands
next to this woman and shouts across to me: 'Hey
broer, she says she wants me, what do you say?'
I suggest that he let her have him. He then says:
'No, she has expired. I mean when she was still
fresh i wanted her but she refused. Now that she
is past her expiry date she comes running...'

SEKGONYAMATLHO... the brew that gouges the eyes out. None of the drinkers knows what goes into the making of this concoction. Some say among the ingredients: head of dead dog, battery acid... if none, then methylated spirits, also known as 'blue train', King Korn, yeast... and then it is said also the brewer's bathwater after use, especially after the vaginal wash, when 'bush has been douched', even menses,and that is when it is at its yummiest. In places it is known as 'uhamba nobani' – who are you with. Because if alone, you do not get served. Reason being it is so heavy, one needs a crutch in the form of a fellow drinker afterwards, to walk home. Other places still, 'mokoko-o-ntjhebile' meaning 'the cock is watching me', owing to the hallucinatory nature of the effects. A potent, murderous liquid that makes the colour run out of the skin and grey rise to the surface. The eyes go dull, blood around the black sun in the middle.

It is syphilitic here. A decaying presence hangs over the place. Like something has been dying for a while. & keeps on. Pus flowing from every orifice. Paradise forest, sold by lies. Deception keeps the tourists coming. The veneer of it. The wind through the bush. Yes at night the stars come to rest on the visitor's head and a dreamy quality comes over you. 'The water is sweetest here', the tour-talk sales prattle goes. But raw

sewage flows thick through the taps around here.
At least water for the township. The farmlands
get their water from deep in the earth and off
the Marico River. The dweller in the coop... well,
the municipality's whim with chemicals decides
between sickness and health.

Primary school children carry plastic bottles of
Sekgonyamatlho to school, hide it up in a tree.
All through the day they keep running out of
class and coming back looking 'livelier'. & then
the mother is called to school and she goes to get
her own morning supply before going to see the
principal or whoever has called her. By the time
she hits the gate her mouth is more mobile than
her legs. Announces her arrival outside the school
gate with expletives, a proficiency in the use of
abdominal references directed at whatever forces
of authority reside within. Swearing as out of the
deepest void.

*

*I had a record on the Technics 1210 & the damned
cat thought of diversion, jumped on the vinyl
wanting to DJ. Not the kind of scratching that
DJ Premier would approve of. Then i brought an
LP home, sat it on the carpet while hooking up
the machine & the dog came in and pissed on it.
I guess a statement of criticism of the album. In
total or just the liner notes? Perhaps the notes
within?*

Children get pregnant in their numbers. Adults
sex children with their parents' consent. The
spermers more often than not their fathers' age.
Mention it and it's enmity turf. Talk ill of it at
your peril: 'He is her man, he takes care of her...
Who are you?... hm... Will you feed her if you say
she must not lie with him?' Numerous assaults,
plentiful wounds have come of such.

'Ah, the Whites protect their property' says the
social worker. Referring to the white males who
come for carnal pleasures in the township, get
children pregnant... well, they pay for their seed.
And all is good. Blessed baas.

The Department of Health distributes
prophylactics, for free. Within an hour of its van
departing, condoms are strewn all across the

township. Toddlers blow them up for balloons.

Social grant. R300 per child. Grant day is a
party. First though, groceries. 1kg sugar, 2.5kg
maize meal and that is it, until next month. The
shebeen is fun-time teeming. Mad laughter and
loves. Dancing dust-up. And the toilets overflow
and waste streams out. Babies on backs. Next
day, next to the condoms, the blood, faecal
matter... disposable diapers.

The school provides a bus, rickety, rusted,
paint-peeling but locomoting well from corner to
schoolyard. Transport there and back, for free.
Feeding scheme serves lunch of brown bread,
peanut butter and skimmed milk... bell ring,
assembly prayer and stomach grumbles. Within
minutes of school starting the child, dressed in
a shirt a week's dirt-clogged because no soap,
sweated in until the stench stayed, and faded,
onto the skin, asks 'Teacher, when are we eating?'
The child went to bed hungry, and woke with
hunger, and came to class.

The Superior In-breeds – entire families, granny
mother aunt daughter grandchildren all twisted
up, drool laden faces squashed in on themselves
like someone trying to kiss themselves... the
attitude of supremacy, still... they call the Black
a primate who should be made to 'fear the night

again, like with our ancestors... you are the
only white tribe in the world to stand for these
animals... it is a disgrace... god gave us dominion
over these stinky sheep... we need to take the
ground back, bit by flesh-bought bit... as we
move back to the western province' their kin
say. They are already there, where the sun sets.
Visages warped. Like sick. Vomit bubbling under
the facial surface. The pallor a cross between
carroty and banana-tinge... Theo, in between
singing the praises of his 'Viking forebears, why
i stand close to seven feet' says 'you know we
used to be ashamed, we had a national shame, us
Afrikaners... of breeding with our own daughters
and sisters. But that time is gone, no more.'
Across the Marico street dust, the in-bred family
crawls. He looks aside. Like willing me not to see
them.

When Pauline sits down, her dog, it is close to the
earth, short and long, i call it Tapyt... it is never
washed, dusty, has the smell of wet dirt on fur...
it smells from a distance... well, when she sinks
down to her seat the dog jumps up next to her
and muzzles up, inching its nose deep between
her legs, into her crotch. And she doesn't seem
to notice its pink penis-head sneaking out of its
woollen scabbard. I want to throw up.

LELEME has been working for Fantasma and

Albert since he was 15, that was 25 years ago. He earns R1200. She got him out of school, he says. Makes up for his feelings of emasculation by baas-boying his fellow workers. Part of it comes from... well, since baas is so brittle, shaman-fragile he doesn't walk, not even shuffle, he breeze-floats and settles light as dust on marula, his stomach-length beard butterflying before him... and missus shakes the earth when she walks, boundless, inexhaustible... well, baas really can't keep up so Leleme is a walking-talking human dildo. Perhaps that is why he is the lackey, telling on his fellow workers to his madam. Runs things in the fields like he owns them, and maybe he does, by dong-right.

'Them bitches' tongues come unfurled', said Bushwick Bill. And i think of the road ahead, trying to raise the race. Hard when the Geto Boys thump through the speakers, their hard man Willie D snarling: 'preaching that positive shit that you can keep/ cos your positivity aint getting motherfuckers paid!'

Miscegenation times... what is slime in the 'holy books' of pigmentation is loin-rhyme out of church and ideology. The colour codes that rule.

And Mista Doty says: 'They ask me what happens to the foreskins after they get cut. Well, they are

useful. We sew them together into a handbag.
See, when you have to travel you just rub it up
and it becomes a suitcase. Watch out for the
rain, though...' further and further... 'I caught
my son masturbating in the bath yesterday...
asked him what the hell he was doing and he said
'it is mine, i can wash it as fast as i want'... 'he
dreamed he was peeping on the girl in the flat
across the tracks from his window... she was lying
there naked, and his dick started travelling, you
know... going to her... crept across the rail lines
and climbed up the wall... and just when it was
about to slide in he heard the sound of the train,
coming... you should have seen him reeling his
cock back... and the train came hurtling down...
he screamed... and woke up.'

Fluffy, strengthless hair of malnutrition. Brittle
stick figures.Their colours greying. Sickly
brown runny underneath, peeping out. The gait
unsteady. Windblown, as if about to topple over.
Watery eyes. Dusty ankles.

Wall of poverty closing in... all a mendicant...
father mother children, can't tell, kids speaking
in faded adult tones... impoverishment early
given to defilement.

Truck stops otherside the street – a teenage
had her thumb out this side, standing next to a

grown woman, baby on back. Gal walks across
the street, head turned up to the driver's window,
woman shouts across: 'don't forget to get the
money first, before anyone...'

We drive past, group of pre-teens... one shouts: 'ke
kope ranta, mosadi!' (give me a rand, woman!') ...
sounding like her grandmother.

Mista VEG is pink-faced, heavy-breathing and weighs about 200kg. He drives a truck laden with farm vegetables. He goes up and down the streets and stops at intervals and people gather around the truck and buy. Mornings he does his route and afternoons parks opposite the post office and just sits in his car. After a while one black teenage girl or another walks up to the car, climbs in. & off the truck drives. Hours later it comes back and the girl gets deposited at the same place. & walks off carrying a plastic bag brimming with onions, green beans, peppers and other veggies. & the look on the teen's face as she passes is defiant, like daring you to say anything about it. Today though, another girl shouts across the street: 'Hey, you, what are you doing with my property? Be careful, i will scratch your face.' And the one freshly off the truck voices off: 'Mista veg is not mine, sister... he is ours. We share him.' She steps up to the other and they disappear into the shop. Sisters in miscegenated paedophilia.

Why fuck what you deem beneath you? No pun.
If so inferior, filthy, sub-human, bestial... why
copulate with 'it'? Pink loins on fire... the race of
desire... lust gone bust... once below the waist,
racism goes to waste... the closer the groping of it,
the more progressive i guess.

GRANDPA TELKOM and the brother who's kept his judgement for oblivion. 'I am scared to speak. I don't want to end up at The Flag,' says the brother, bowing his head under the heckling derision of his fellow workers at the bottle-store. & in the afternoon bushveld sun, the trees yellowing in the heaviness of it all, the beer goes down heavy, sits rock-hard on the stomach. His little sister has just stepped out of the van with Telkom scrawled across its side. In the driver's seat sits a fawn-complexioned old man who could have been her great-grandfather. The brother says he knows the old man sexes her, and the family knows too. They let it go. And he zips his snout up. She might take him to prison-land should he speak out.

Starvation, dehydration... the water, when and if it comes, not often chocolate-coloured, of faecal complexion, truer even... i'm looking at death by immurement.

'Ga re tshabe makgoa, rona' – song and dance children of the dust... marimba squad, they get pushed to the fore in loincloths for the tourist season. I hear them proclaim their lack of fear of the whiteness of the land-rule. They are not like their parents, each twelve-year-old of them says. But they play their percussions, and dance, and play 'native'. Their tips get sliced in half by the lady organiser of the tourist office. She says the half she takes is for their future use. She owns a game farm.

SASSA days – the shebeen – wretched humanity – social granted a stamp to perennial debt –

> *Give you the 6 foot... cough in it. Coffin shit.*
> *The truth of the mad hatter*
> *Is... how the subject matters*
> *to the crown/clown.*
> *(tongue in chick. thinking of Cunnilinguists...*
> *hip hop heirs to the bop.*
> *'I speak here... of... nomenclature...'*
> *'sorry, can't help you. I don't know any Norman*
> *Clutcher or whatever his name is...'*

THE MAN WHO KILLED THAMI MNYELE lives on a farm down the road with baboon-skulls on the gate. People here say he is a mass murderer.

Psychedelic storm – the skies are HENDRIXIAN.

CATCH THEM WHILE THEY ARE YOUNG, and they do. The truck-drivers going their cross-country routes. & they pay the girl-children to splay themselves and get stuck, and afterwards you see them, the children, slink into the Indian shop and get bread, jam and milk. There will be food at home that night.

LEE the transgendered gay coloured boy-girl
hustler: 'The more manly butch rugby bier-en-
boerewors aggro-types are always the first to
throw their legs over their heads. It works for
me because even though on the outside i am a
boy-girl, in the bedroom i am the alpha male... at
home they are expected to be strong, overbearing,
providing, very manlik... but inside they just
want to be fucked by big black cock, and me,
well, i am not black enough but what can they
do, you know? You would be surprised how
many of them fantasise about just spreading and
taking that swartpiel... I have not been without
lovers in Madikwe... that man who owns half
the restaurant on the N4, he is married and
everything, to that ultra-racist woman, well...
he was my lover for the first three months i was
here...'

'In the mornings they drive their wives to work,
eyes straight ahead stuck on the road, but
afternoons when they come back, you should see
how slowly they cruise past here, hoping to see
my arse in high heels in the garden... we party,
and we are not serving koeksusters here, doll...
well, it starts with brandy and coke and then
somewhere down the line someone accidently does
something and by then your senses are swimming

around and then someone puts something in your mouth... and hoo, can you imagine my legs up high on the wall and high heels and i shag deep, baby hoo... you know for the boers with all that macho stuff it is easier to come out as gay than as a vegetarian... odd, hey?' Lee continues: 'After the sin-breeding... in-bredding... that is, the incest, the seed turning inward, the deep-rooted cross-race homosexual urges hiding beneath the boer-bull mask is the Afrikaner's greatest secret. Ask me, i know, i have fucked more than enough of the straight raging racists...'

& then they killed Lee. To keep it all hidden. Maybe it came out of double/triple/more-dick-parking. Maybe jealousy. Or just... well, it was another Vlakplaas on a Madikwe farm. His boer-lovers chopped him up & fed him to the flames while they swilled the famed brandy-and-coke. & he burned through the night. & the sunrise was bushveld beautiful as always.

Snap–spine
crackle-heart
then again... pop-eyeballs
Come in wearing a cardiac-vest?
It pierces thru, that Black magic like
voodoo-needle.
Life is improvisation.
Soloing in and out of existence
The devil's own reticence
me and him in rhythm...
I'm riffing off Scott-Heron

THAPELO BEATDOWN – I walked the dusty,
mud-watery streets of Seding to Thapelo's
home. Looks and stares all around. The anger,
frustration, disappointment, betrayal must have
shown purple on my face. I strode, warpath
mapped out. To his sickly father putting his torn
shirt on over his protruding rib-cage as i turned
the last corner to his yard. He glanced furtively
around and i saw his younger son run into the
house and close the curtains. No matter. The
man's voice, tiny, brittle, fragile with illness,
the cheekbones cutting into the fleshless skin
on his mask-face, his nose dripping, eyes off the
sockets... i had bought food for him, was waiting
for money to get his children school uniforms... he
looked at me and turned away. And shuffled.

Words were not plenty. I said: 'Your child is going to die. You would too, this minute, but you are on your way anyway. You don't love your children, you wouldn't lie otherwise... I came here, and you looked at me, in the eyes, deep, talking about your pain, and then shit-faced said your child had not stolen my things, he was here the whole time. People saw him run out of my place, with my things. They know him, he grew up among them, they had faith in you too, like the woman who works at the shop. She says she called out to him when he ran past, carrying things in his arms and he pretended not to hear, did not even give a look back. And i trusted you, came to you and you lied.' I see the little boy, Thapelo's brother, break into a smile when he thinks i am not looking.

Then Thapelo turns the corner, dressed in a new shirt. & he comes up all angelic smiles. & i hit him hard, side of the face, and he spins around and crashes into a muddy puddle. & the shirt catches it. & i lift him by the shirt front and hit him again. The light flashes white in my eyes as he thumps back in the dust. & as he lifts his head and i prepare to stomp on it, i see beneath his head, a brick... and i know, in that instant, my shoe on his face and his skull would crack. & i see him try catch a string of brain ebbing out, and a blood-line writing its way into the earth... into the mud and dust. & i know... this is death

waiting. I return my foot back to land... turn,
look at the father, he stands there, arms folded.
The little boy is looking too, blank-faced. I look
at Thapelo screaming out 'it wasn't me!' I know
he lies. Like his father. And that he is laughing,
like his brother. And i feel defeat. I turn and walk
away. People are out of their yards, standing in
the street, getting entertained. I walk away.

Don't ask me anything regarding music. I
know nothing about it. Thank you. Like U-Roy:
'lyrics... / addicted to music... / hear when me
seh I could never refuse it... / i'm addict / gawd! /
i'm a music addict / lawd!' No junkie 'knows' the
drugs they are on. Props and Reachers. The Hype.
Fashion accessories for the arm but never the
bandstand. They look good so the refracted gleam
falls on the musician. They would be hangers-on if
at the play-end the music-maker wasn't so beat he
had to hang on, drape himself around them. They
are more like hangers, then. Home to the artists,
who are the plungers. Like in a pool, or a toilet-
bowl. Flip it in the other direction: they are also
the poison. Mortal coil unfold, check under the
bed, or in the closet & they are there.

James Phillips at Jameson's, coming off stage in
all passion-held weariness, hitching his guitar up
against disillusion, looks over the post-musical
mess at their Colgate-toothed love, & whispers his
exhaustion: 'they do not get enough until there is
nothing left to be given...'

'Praat Afrikaans of hou jou bek!'
Nazi farmers spout superiority.

The Germans cometh – the volunteer students

knobbing black – the farmers march – send a
delegation to the embassy – thou shalt not fuck
kaffir!

Pauline claims progressiveness & so does her
engineer husband. Go to their house & meet the
unwashed bodies, heavy stench, the pig-weight
sitting heavy – green the water in the sink
stacked with the filth of last week's unwashed
plates, to report sighting of a car accident. 'What
race was the driver? ... You know they raped a
white woman – in Zeerust they killed a white old
couple...' First the pigmentation, that will provide
explanation, give reason, & all else will follow.
The guiding principle for the weighing of human
worth.

CHINA CHILD, SHEBEEN MOM. FATHER
GOT HERE SOMEHOW. They own the shebeen,
mom & dad. Within a month of his arrival they'd
hooked up. He speaks Mandarin, strictly. Her
tongue is Setswana, only. They communicate
in... BODY. Their child is now learning to walk.
& talk. Wonder to watch as they try one to grab
the other's words out of the air as they fly over, &
above. They call it Love. Mzamane named such
'animal instinct'. Their story is getting mixed
in with the MADIKWE MYTHS like the water
snake heralding the EVIL core BENEATH the
TRANQUILITY cosmetics that get splashed

across the Tourism Board's brochures selling the clean living pure air breathed before the oink factor shows face.

A series of terrible noises from up the tree opposite. For quite a while. I am used to gunshots. These bush-sounds... no. So i locked my doors, closed my windows. I could hear my AWB neighbour in hysterics, yapping fast in Afrikaans (on the phone, i found out later)... anyway after a bit a police van came screeching into my yard. fok, i forgot the noises in the tree and thought 'oh damn, there we go again, they are here to get me'... but then no, they ran into the cluster of trees and started screaming: 'shoo, klim af, gaan by julle', clapping their hands all the while. My neighbour piped in: 'Hy moet weg gaan, hy gaan my honde afval... hy soek hul kos.' Hell no, she starves the blasted things. I am forced to feed them on the sly. She caught me at it once. Anyway, they replied: 'It is just a monkey up there. No harm. These type monkeys do not attack dogs, harmless creatures, no danger at all.'

I waited till all the noise died down, no more screeches and shouts, before i opened my door. Hell no, what do I know about monkeys. Fok, gimme Okapis and pangas any day... ah well... another Marico day. By now my neighbor must be knowing not to rely on me for ANY help on

ANY matter whatsoever. Her dogs are full of
complaints, they say her AWBism has grown
deeper since her husband ran off with that
Motswana woman. The dogs want out, their
sensibilities are being polluted, they say. Time to
break out... thus it is you see me running around
trying to get a pair of wire-cutters.

USED CONDOMS & soiled diapers... shake-
shake khatuns... i am stocktaking in the bush.
Amid human faeces and dead birds, fighting
with stray dogs for space, in the night and
drunkenness people couple there. And leave
trails.

Sitting in the taxi yesterday, en route to the
Marico. These two mature ladies start talking
about a man they are afraid of. You wouldn't
think it of him as he 'smells of water'. But see,
he turns himself into a neckless chicken when
the police come looking for him, on account of
his dagga-peddling activities. On top of that,
though, and in the service of the community...
say, for instance, someone steals from you. Well,
you go to mista 'neckless chicken', he inflates a
soccer-ball and oh oh, the thief starts bloating up,
swelling outward, with the accompanying pain,
of course, wherever s/he is, getting really large,
outrageously so. Should they then repent and
bring your stolen property back, and of course if

you are in a forgiving mood, you go back to mista 'neckless chicken', he deflates the soccer-ball and with a loud, gigantic fart the thief whooshes right back to his original size. Gore-dam. I now understand the Daily Sun.

*

*CHARLES MINGUS Ah Um... like Overture with
an upright. Rebel-axeman. Insurrection-time.*

*Ornette got mass-divisive to self-define. Miles
walking his croak like lightning-strike but still, oh
delicate, god. Not many more... not playing bon-
bons. They scratch the chicken.*

*Let them sleep who are tired.
Beam me back to '59. Jazzing it up in Revolution
line and time. We are wired.
They mourn Bird by ingesting heroin. His be-
bopping buddies.*

THE R5 MAN: 'We do not live well, today, on the
wall...' He comes up to me, sitting on a low sofa
with the covering gone over the cushion. Resting
against the wall of the liquor store. 'They have
changed things, up in the head, the people i live
with. They were not like this, handling me in
this bad manner. It is my mother-in-law's house
we are living in. You could look at us & think we
are having a good life, no, you would be wrong.
When they eat i just sit there, watching them.
There is no plate for me. Even in the morning
they drink their tea & just look at me like i am
not even there. i watch them feed. & i say this
is not how we live, where i come from... i am

from Hartebees. My people are there. Life is no longer good, here... hey, don't you have R5 for me, please. Some people said they would help me & i was happy but then they said i must go to them in Zeerust... you know, i hate Cape Town, you know why? There you can walk the whole day & not see one stompie to smoke. Here it is better...'

Rough, dry cough wracks him until his body shakes. In the middle of it he digs into his frayed jacket, pulls out a small plastic bag filled with cigarette stubs, most of them smoked close to the filter, different brands. He digs into his pants pocket & out with a strip of newspaper. Sores twin-lines along his lips, his trousers are stuck, in places, holding tight to his legs. A yellow-green colour & a sour odour coming off the sticking. Something festered in there. Septic. Purulent. Like gangrene. The sickness is deeper than the surface rot, something says. 'I used to work on the mines. Platinum. It left my insides... numb.' I think of a sick, retarded beast.

He starts milking the stubs of the little tobacco lodged behind the burnt ends, onto the paper. A little pile forms. Getting bigger. In the end he has quite a bit, a lot of it black. There is some brown, though. He works the pile with care into enough for a joint. He wets the length of it with his tongue. Searches for a matchbox, shakes it,

tiny sound from within. One matchstick. Works
the flint. With a flourish, lights. Inhales, blows
a couple of fancy smoke rings & leans back with
some satisfaction. Takes a few drags. 'Ah, let me
haul myself away. Don't worry, you can help me
another day. Be blessed.' He goes away, dragging
his skinny frame, it seems. In his old, ragged
Pringle jacket, Arrow shirt underneath, Stetson
hat so threadbare you can see the shiny black
beneath the brown, Crockett & Jones shoes with
the heels gone. Leaves me with questions. He
used to be the best dressed chicken in town, from
the look of things. 'Can't remember most of the
places i have been to. When i did. Whom with,
mostly. The years around & into the spaces &
the other way. Faces, bodies, too. Minds... not
so much.' That's the lore-skin, cut... get to the
shaft... deeper than myth, go... flip that back, & it
is theme... music to your film.

Mountains range the landscape. Make the
mind feel shut in, bush-logged & locked green.
Patchwork of yellowish-light brown dotted like
patches on the head, ring-wormed, that rock.
Sight of a lone dirt-road winding & running
up until it disappears. A steep decline there. &
the mountain growing large from there. Still a
distance. The N4 freeway cuts through this side,
down it a T-junction, beginnings of what becomes
the dirt-road. Cut across, past the sign that

reads: 'ABORTION. Safe & pain-free. WOMB CLEANING. Dr Joy'... & the doctor's phone-numbers. It is rental floss. Fleece.

I had a small studio, once. Non-music lovers raided it. 'Drop the words out', like Louis Moholo said at Brotfabriek, Zurich, angry with me constantly 'sitting on the beat': 'that is the problem with jazz-groupies, you guys never let the music breathe.'

No one rhythm-thread is worth dwelling on 'too long'. That is, past whatever purpose it intends serving. 'Keep it moving' is my governing principle.

ABEL is the potential salvation of this place. The only person i meet i can talk books with. He writes, & well too. He says he feels 'out of place in the township. & at that water resource spot where i work. You know when you want to discuss things people don't get, don't want to, no interest. You start feeling like you are forcing issues... so i just lock myself up. Read my books. & write. Talk to myself. But now i have you. Look, this is my thought. Most South African literature is dead. Across race, genre, generation... i draw no inspiration from it. I am not knocking people but stating what is to me, as writer and avid reader, a fact. This to me is a jump-off point. I did not come into writing because some SA writer fried my brains, but precisely because they did not. I wished for more. Starting out, I wrote because i could not stand what i was reading – uniform in its dearth of imagination, i felt like i was locked behind a marshmallow wall. The padding could be eaten from here to sugar diabetes...'

Abel continues: 'Madikwe is so under-represented in SA popular imagination it is criminal. In many ways it is the microcosm of the country. All the forces, human & otherwise, are here. Or come to dip their sticks in these waters. Its superficial presentation, the tranquil face, hides much that is beyond ugly. An aged white man in shorts, the veins standing green on his pallid legs, said that, in a queue at the post office while overhearing me praise the quiet, the air that actually does flow around here, the stars coming down at night. Madikwe incorporates the country's deep beauty & pointless, immediate brutality.'

THE ALCOHOL FLOWS & Abel's passion rises: 'Herman Charles Bosman – bushveld writing... both Vooorkamer & oom Schalk Lourens... he is my main man. Brother of Makana, lover of the land, yes, still... Bosman's blacks, like the Vietnamese in Hollywood depiction... Platoon, Apocalypse Now, Deer Hunter... are really just ciphers. Boat-people outside, almost, of the field

of vision. Never really central, or felt, even.
Prejudices are bounced against, the ignorance of
the perpetrators thrown at them, but they are
never really characters, people, themselves, the
victims of such. Even though the intention is to
show up the throwers, better yet, the tossers...
can't you imagine them standing in the wind one
hand pumping... must be why the flowers refuse
to grow in the bushveld, acid-sperm kills them.'
He pours bourbon to the top of his glass. Who
knows it might be the last i offer him. 'Publishers
manufacture writers for us, award-winning
creatures, you speak to some of these people &
it is clear they can't have written the books that
bear their damn names. It is a scam.'

Abel lives beyond the sign by the roadside that
says:

> *Another Human Settlement development*
> *Construction of 600 sustainable human*
> *settlements units*
> *No of units: 600 Land size: 53 hectares*
> *Project value R 696 720 000*
> *Typology: rural development Jobs created: 300*
> *"Working Together We Can Do More"*
> *Dept Human Settlements Rep. of South Africa*
> *Anti-corruption phone number: 0800 00 28 70*

JUST BEYOND THIS SIGN, a few metres after
turning left, is the entrance to Loop en Val Sport
Bar & Restaurant
BUCKET list & ICE BEER
SLOW DOWN BAR AHEAD
¼ cheeeeeken served wiff Bunn coleslaw & chips
R49

... a disused Morris mini, yellow, the top gone.
Abel never goes there, he cannot afford it. We are
only here because i offered.

DADDY U ROY (closest to Botswana's Ratsie
Setlhako in terms of phrasing) swinging on the
beat albeit to a drum & bass-driven riddim.
The Motswana had used the Segaba, a bow
instrument. One wire leading down to a calabash,
played with a length of wire. AFRICAN relative &
forerunner to the euro violin.

'Don't distress it... never you bore a hole in one
riddim.'
– Josey WALES, reggae dj, calling on the band
for a different riddim to be played because they
had been playing one for a while, even though
the audience was enjoying it. 'SOUNDING THE
PAGE' is what i want to call it.

You realise that the graveyard has expanded its
reach, it is moving in, from the outskirts now it
is climbing onto people's backyards. & someone
says: 'Very soon it will go on & up to the rooftops.
& that is where the corpses will be placed, the
dead will rest there, above the houses... will
be laid to rest looking out. Yes, overlooking,
overseeing things. Is that not what badimo do?'

A young guy working at the filling station tells
me: 'Uncle, what works in this place is... sex.
If you have a job, there is not a day you can go

without a woman... People use their bodies here.
And you know the deaths that brings.'

Back at the liquor place, across the freeway from
Loop en Val. Always when i go there, the little,
short man who works there, in his maroon t-shirt
with the blah blah liquor emblazoned onto his
pocket & jeans, is talking to the one who works
next door, in the scrapyard, suffering from a
great stutter-problem but always the one holding
the invisible microphone. I have heard him give
advice to people who have brought their metal
there to sell, while he prepares the industrial
scales: 'Squash it, that will make it weigh more'.
The two always engage me in animated talk, the
reason seems to be that sometimes i buy a couple
of bottles for us.

I look across the way, there's a young man in his
German machine and the woman leaning against
the car opening her zip & showing him her pubis
while her friend stands behind him & says 'Yeah,
buy us alcohol & she will send you... you know,
she will wrap her pussy around your head &
squeeze...' & the man with his stomach hanging
to just above his knees, nestling on his thighs
saying 'You know these speed limits are stupid,
i mean, the 120 kilometres-per-an-hour on my
machine is not the same as on that rickety Ford
Escort...'

And things get pumping. 'Ah, men call me Bee
Gee but women, well... they say my name is
Razor, no need to ask why... I leave it loose, torn,
cut up, tattered, bleeding in little pieces. & they
come back. Always.' He makes a brazier. An old
metallic wash-tub. Rusty. Paper. Goes behind the
shop, comes back with wood, shaking his head.
A length of wired-fence worked into a square. A
kind of sieve. Gets a fire built... chicken pieces
tossed on the wire. 'We bought them at that
woman, you know Freedom Chicken? Well, their
chickens often trample one another to death.
& they sell the dead ones to her. She pulls the
feathers off, cuts them open, throws the intestines
& stuff out & sells them, clean, R15. Better
than BJ's restaurant over there, oily two piece
chicken R49! What is best? We buy this whole
one for R15. & cook it the way we like it. Unlike
my boss, you know his house in Rustenburg? Oh,
huge house, in the kitchen... fridges everywhere.
& booze, lots of it. Never runs out. & when i am
there... i sleep IN THE HOUSE... hm, inside...'

He looks over for impression made, continues:
'They live Setswana. The problem with him &
his wife, no, they cook meat and eat it with the
blood still on it. Shit, can you imagine? Man,
no! & when they give me food it's like they are
chasing me away. Liquor, yes, give me heaps but
food... so i say oh, put it in a bag for me, i will

take it home. & when i get there i cook it, long &
proper the Black way. See, that is why his ankles
are swollen, they are like this, have you seen an
elephant, like that. They say it's cancer. No, it
is the half-cooked meat they eat... what white
man do you work for... does he put the meat on
the stove 'til it's proper, cooked, to the bone? No,
see?' I remember Macka B's 'food scandal' raga
joint, & smile. Wriggling toes like granny. To the
soundless riddim-track in my head.

In the hair-salon, my people's sign:
TRETEMENT-R40
COULOUR-R60
FREEZ-R50
DABRET-R100
WOOL STYL-R130
POMEDY-R60
EXTENTION TONG-60
TO START DREAD-R300
SOFT DREADS-R150
YAKI-R200
BIG BRUSH AMERICAIN-R25
PLATING REMOVAL-R30/80
WASH AFRO-R45
WASH EXTENTION-R50

Whoever said that the Nigerians and Jamaicans
have us beat in administering blows to that
queen's yap?

Riding WITH RHYTHM DEEP WITHIN.
Johnny Dyani said: 'Music must have a rhythm.
I'm fed up with this avant-garde that says you
must have no time. I want a rhythm I can relate
to because any move anyone makes has rhythm –
some is graceless and some is informed by grace,
but it's the rhythm of life. People in Europe don't
identify with the drum or relate to drum culture
and that's a pity.'

And Dudu Pukwana maintained: 'You can't play
without time. Time is there, it's natural, like day
and night. There's a drum inside you, while it
keeps on pumping it keeps on living and that's
time too.'

Innate rhythm, a sense of 'time' in the words
falling.

Writing notes, my beer bottle by my side, snug
on the coverless cushion. A huge police truck
pulls up, one policeman alone in the truck. Sgt
Oink i call him since he tried some intimidation
moves on me & i promised to puncture his balls.
He stares at me, climbs out, i continue writing,
look up when he is a metre away, gauging the
distance to my bottle. Thinking i can slice off half
his child-bearing hips from where i sit if he comes

any closer. He pulls his nose up, trying to have it touch his hair-line. Looking like Porky without all that greasiness, he gives an even uglier impression. I look him in his repulsive mug & he walks past. Starts throwing fat weight on the scrapman, claims he has been receiving, paying for & moving stolen scrap-metal. Last week the police arrested the white boy whose family own the place, he spent two nights at The Flag. It is said the competition is behind it. I never knew scrap could be contraband. i sit there, write, take a swig. I hope Oink remembers i promised to chop off his raisins. He pretends i no longer exist. Suits me. Rolls his watery buttocks back into the truck & makes it roar, over-revving for effect, not looking at me all the while. Screeches tyres while making off. I scribble on.

They roll in their scrap-metal. Two shrunken black 'til blue-in-the-face women, the faces themselves showing evidence of years of alcohol tracks and violence – the one's jaws are twisted out of shape & extra-long, hanging to the left. They find a younger one, no older than 17, the scrap-metal man thinks 19, rather. She is in whispered talk with an older man. They disappear behind the building. Elephant grass there, people often go there to urinate. The women sit there, they are owed for metal they brought three days ago, they have lost the receipt.

The scrapman keeps them hanging, they sit for
an hour. Says one to the other while they wait for
their young friend to get back from her business:
'Lift your skirt like this. Over your head. & show
them what you've got. They will give us R4. We
want to go drink strong...'
'You must open wide...'
'You know she had her legs so open & there was
not even an itjhuu coming out of her mouth. So
young, and him so older. Oh what he had, shoo, i
had to close my one shot, two balls.
Razor & Scrapman at the snooker table.

Across the way the women: 'I don't sell body. I
have a man.'

'Nnyo ya R20, no no no... R20 for cunt. Not
happening. Not even R50, i won't give it to him. &
worse when i know he has a drum in those pants
& i agree? Never in hell... He must forget. But
this girl does not know what no is, it is always
yes, anything for cents, not with me.'

PPC CEMENT, STRENGTH GUARANTEED.
The lorry rolls past. Earlier, this white man in a
van, had said it reminded him of himself: 'That
is me, my friend. Look, i can sex, me. My wife
knows it. I am fokken heavy, me.' He had been
alternating between screaming, bragging &
exhibitions of race-arrogance: 'Hey, where's the

rest of my change? This Three Ships is R222.90, i gave you R223. I am a millionaire, me. You don't give me my shilling i take all my money back. Simple. I will buy somewhere else. Down the road here.' He always comes here with his one worker in the passenger seat. Will never himself go into the shop, being so fat it would take a long time for him. But he does not trust his worker to go into the bottle store with his money. He shouts across for Bee Gee Razor to come out, up the window, take the money & the order, go back inside, get the alcohol & bring it out. & the change is always an argument-starter.

From somewhere, words: 'They stuck a gun up his arse, pulled the trigger & you could see the shit shoot out of his mouth'. & now Razor sings a song: 'Don't be a bull to other people's children.' & the women giggle. Getting more agitated by the minute until i dip in my pocket because they have been saying: no, just give us R4, you can pay us the rest of the R23 later, so that we can go have some JIJA. I ask what that is & get told by scrapman it is a perversion of GINGER. Refers to the deadly concoction whose base is ginger powder, otherwise known as SEKGONYAMATLHO around these parts. Poor people's entertainment. Like sex. I have seen that. & people on it.

The other woman reappears, her male company not. She smiles. They leave, with haste. Already feeling the taste of it. I will miss the talk when even my skin shrinks & turns inward.

Half an hour passes, the disappeared man comes stumbling from behind the building, zipping up. Says: 'No,man. Sy is flenter, daai kind. There is nothing there left. Niks. No grip, nothing. It is like swimming in mud. No feeling, nothing. The muscles are nowhere in there. Ek nodig nie selke goed weer. I am not the one for it. I don't want her stukkend poes ever again. Fok. It is amen.' Minutes later the young woman reappears, enraged, shouts at him: 'Hey wena, i want my poes-money!'

*

DUB –
Kodwo Eshun:
As soon as you have echo, listening has to
completely change.

LEE SCRATCH PERRY – science of the mixing
board:
'I put my mind into the machine and the machine
performs reality.'

This music is... description & being... of place
& character is supreme. The language use true.
Salvages dignity & a deep humanity from the
misery & human degradation & wreckage. A sense
of lived reality.

I grab my bag, stick the rest of my provisions
in my rucksack, & head off homeward. Halfway
there, the sun coming on dead-weight top of the
head, a 4x4 van comes down the road. Two white
men inside. Metres away from me the driver
swings it hard & off the road & onto the dust-
track i am on & then twists the wheel hard & off
& back on to the road & the passenger shrieks,
laughing. I shout 'What the fuck's that? Pale pig
shit arse!' & stick my fuck-your-mother-finger
up high. I catch the driver's face in the rear-view

mirror, the van hurtling away. No rocks around, i
would have smashed the back-window. Moments
like this i miss my Okapi. Fine, reliable, user-
friendly knife, that.

I traverse the deserted streets. Later, shadows
swallowing things up. The place's orifices,
entrance & exit points. Looking for the khakis in
their war-van. The circus is nowhere showing.
I carry myself home. Breathing hard. The war
abandoned mid-march. It turns within. Someone's
out there playing a trumpet in the twilight. I
can't see them for the bush. Might be a serenade.
Bosman said the moon does strange things to
people here, like making them romantic.

Reminds me of Theo. He came to live in what
used to be the servants' quarters. He was always
on my case with stupid jokes about how the
native is now in the 'big house' and ex-baas in
the 'girl's room'. & he would crack up. I suspected
something venomously bitter beneath the
laughter. He would constantly talk about how
not racist he was. THE ORGANISATION that
put me here got him there, his brother sits on the
committee. He came from the Cape, had stories of
smoking marijuana with Rastas.

One early evening he came at me, frothing about
how he was a descendant of Vikings and could

smash anything to dust. By which he meant me.
He stood about a metre taller than me, and i am
not a midget. He was swinging, wildly. I snaked
hand into my pocket & pulled out my Okapi,
it glistened in the moonlight. It flashed a few
centimetres close to his chest, once twice. He laid
the gate flat, running. He crashed through the
bushes and was gone. The next day the committee
called me to a meeting, saying he was blabbering,
eyes wide, could hardly register, what had i done?
I said i had just got so scared i reached into my
pocket in a panic, for my cellphone. It is shiny,
the phone. I wanted to call one of them because i
thought the giant was going to kill me. They said
he mentioned a knife. I said i could understand
that. In the light of that moon a shiny phone
could be mistaken for a knife. I never saw him
again.

I am still here. & the moon is up there. & some
toneless person is playing the trumpet. In the
gathering gloom. & if i ever heard an elephant
fart, no, a rhino, in the water, like some people
play the piano as they do, letting their bowels
loose to evict the wind that 'has not paid the rent',
as Rockwell puts it. It would sound just like that
trumpet, i think. Then the muezzin from across
the way kicks in. & this early evening i imagine
some infidel clutching the muezzin's testicles
tight in a vice-grip, not letting the balls drop until

the chanting is done. The mosque is behind the
trees too. I thank whatever god. & behind the
trees on the other side of the house comes the
tinny, dissonant, ear-piercing-because-so-sharp
one-beat noises of the shebeen's juke-box. I am
surrounded. Even the mini-fridge in the kitchen
hums, 1000 bees-power, it sounds like. Scraping
the walls & the floor of my eardrums. Chalk on
blackboard. Knife on tar/ concrete. Water-torture.
These images have been used before, that doesn't
make them invalid. I am in the sonic-middle.
Field of concentration. Heavy flatulent sonar-
artillery. Writing this, the paper starts cackling
away, the pen's screech burning rubber i can
even smell the ink. Mockery. I scratch my head in
frustration and nails on scalp are a cement-gravel
mixing machine turning. Tinnitus. The Trinity's
Arse. I pop double pills to sleep.

Defection. Like THE GODFATHER OF
G-FUNK, from social class. & defecation on it,
too, ideological allegiances & embraces... Not
always glorious, check Baraka. Of Black Music.
& BLUES PEOPLE. Super-star/trooper-scar...
melanin race to the 'house of the rising sun'.

Reminder: you carry them along with you
regardless of load-shedding.

Reflection eternal? It stinks on & with you... you

sweat it —

the art-makers, unlike fart-shakers, should not
exist above their social milieu.

(This was written on bourbon, beer & cigarettes. A little food & good pussy. Should have been composed in semen on bubble butt-cheeks. A POLLOCK splash of seed across uterine walls. Instead... sensitive, pain-charged like sniper-shot Fikile charcoal & pencil-lines. Figures in praise of black people's beauty. Even with the worms crawling out from within the canvas. I am my art. In it i pound, cardiac.)

JAZZING THE BUSHVELD WAY

THE POLITICS is written into the music. That horn speaks louder than any banner frapping red. It's art attacks crack-piped dreams, tremors, shivering out of pores, hollers, squawks, squeals, shrieks, moans, ecstatic groans, in and out of the church of SELF. Jazz like AMIRI tried make us envision spilling out street dirt heaven-hellward. Surrounds of heaving flesh & thrashing skin flared nostrils & gaping holes. Orifices & openings in the ground. They say there is a Black ore up there.

VUSI XIMBA – maskandi man with a concertina & concerted effort at social-build beyond the Dracula-chest-plate-pierce humorous, dies without respect cos 'to the stake with the conscious artist' rattled tribal out of the race-haunted castle.

*RATSIE SETLHAKO looming over all this, the
father of it all. Setswana microphone killing
– Ratsie Setlhako & his descendants (Culture
Ambassadors, Culture Spears, Matsieng – music
& theatre on vinyl, plus traditional dance –
tshwana & tinto) the past rendered contemporary.*

'Why you coming to the gig drunk, PHILIP?'

*'You, they, all treat me like a machine... well,
machines need oiling otherwise have me play dry
and the music might creak... my pistons get gone.
Stop your talk, I need medicine. No, I have to get
lubrication...' reaches for a brandy straight. &
once plugged in & amped, the sounds are fluid.
Fire-liquid.*

*Another time another crutch... I think Hendrixian
psychedelics. Heroin Birded. Clutch in, breaks off.
gear in one... acceleration out into the otherworld.
KIPPIE climbing from the death-pits all chirpy off
the buzz in the booze.*

*My bushland playlist:
JAZZ MINISTERS: 'Sekumaxa.' For years since
70s coming off the dust of Soweto I hadn't heard
it. Then out of the khaki Bushveld, rustling down
& through the trees til it stirs roots and the leaves*

shake. Leaves my beard breezing in the sonic-
storm. Nostalgia times.

DYANI & BRAND: 'Ntsikana's Bell'. Mbizo hell-
howls & the veins distend chill vibes down the
back, I forget I had a pinched nerve, was it a
slipped disc untwining over that other spinning...
disc-plate.

SAITANA – RUFARO: 'nihuma Joni'... I... come...
am from Johannesburg. I am sin seeking purity in
the bush. The ancestors came out here for roots. &
herbs. Medicinal beyond the chemicals infesting
the Jozi head-&-heartscape.

AFRIKA: 'iyamemeza iAfrika'. He machine flips
it to Side B & 'Mosi oa Thunya you are a hero.'
& I am off my head to Turfloop Emergency
years, teargas & baton-crack-head & the needles
running from ground up after the jump from three
floors up cos the riot police kicked the door in &
detention's not pretty.

MAGWELE: 'Titsoti ta Joni ti ni hlamarisile.'
About Soweto thugs & how he got mugged. & I
remember Phefeni Station, up near the entrance to
the subway. Okapi-flash & then the rattle of bank-
notes punctuated by screams fading off into the
distance behind the heels hitting the back of the
fleeing head.

JOHNNY DYANI: packing Bhaca choirs in the
upright bass. Amabutho arrangements. You
hear the march in the lines. The time is HERE.
Ntsikana's Bell. El the cat sniff-snuffing across the
Bushveld undergrowth. Seeking out man-killing
rats. Biped feline. Piano tinkles and 'reaches the
deeps'... no superstars twinkle here. Humility
immersed within the heavy humidity. Clothes
cling to backs, chests heave, heavy.

Oh, to get to the heart of... things.
Strings need keys to open heartlocks, the natural
mystic, am I romantic?
A dollar for the Mbizo, entrance fee to the
gathering of the spirit tribe.
Open the keyboard you find bloodlines in the
bowels of the piano.
Brand knows this so the fingers are spider kisses
rasping out of gutter note-lips.
Lumps historical in the throats make German
guttural?
Bleed of the music hall was why Mbizo went about
in gumboots (no play)
perhaps so the blood on the dance-hall floor
wouldn't reach through past his
pores... make unheralded entrance.

Technics turntable tricks.
Fables of a hostile past world gone mystical to
birth a new earth?

*Question: between the scratches does the record
itch?
Perry's haunted mixing desk.
Never try modify my high cos in the come-down
I might crack your illusions, shame-ranger.*

*I stopped drinking the fizz sweets when a bee bit
my upper lip. It looked the direct opposite of Louis
Armstrong's with its indentation. Put paid to my
trumpet ambitions. White people put me where I
am. That was Satchmo coming out. Tomming. I
am ever activist. New man, right, Black.*

*They say if you want to hear the Devil speak,
play it Black. That's when the demons screech.
Candomble is Satan's bitch, they believe the Book
inside Vodoun. Santeria is not witches shrieking
but body-sacrecy-sound giving rise to creation.
Freedom-spirit rage-rise in.*

*I watched Sons of Negus play & heard the
Voortrekkers' fear come through in question: 'How
can they march to such a weird beat?' asking of
antiquity, African warriors – speared behind the
shield. No low hide. All exposed & deep into the
flank. All up & down the Rands. Beyond the Day
of the Generals. Crescent moonshine.*

*& the shit flows down the street. They wish
umbrellas around their feet. Or chain-link. But*

the rattle-some is to slavery bound... other...
matter in the Rain, how is it going?

Fire burn.
ORNETTE is the coal-man. Blaze it catch Santa
coming down chimney-town. No diamonds, just
flames on the soles of his feet. He played a plastic
toy-thing and out floated sound so organic it
showed the slave-ship sinking shapes of jazz to
come. Humming heaven down.

The way in is the path home. Weigh in like for the
block at slave auction. The jazz in the spot is hot
but never tourist. You can't buy in. Bloodstains
in the inner notes every... I go in to wash off my
week-day sin. Bird-note springs from his throat
to grab mine. Suffocation, palpitations. I reel out
for write in the spirit. RITE air. Watch granny jus
wiggle her toe... said Mutabaruka, calling out to
the congregants 'Dub in... dub in...'

Kinky Rasta gone drunk inna Babylon. Best place
for that, no fitting, no doubt. All music is thief-
stuff. The lies that bind, we are in jail here, the
man said. Kleptomaniac. The thunder-current
in the singing. Lightning in the picking. Nothing
pastoral cotton heads. PASTORIUS. So real.
Surreal. Seems my human is so bad I always
have to wave a stop-n-go flag saying: 'joke coming,
approach with caution'.

*My up & down beat name of it is aye you won't
know me by looking at my face. Try my bass,
therein you'll find my truth. Walking. Plus every
foetus still all the way in & live... loves BASS. The
unborn kicking? It takes Dub to bring it peace.
The reggae people, they write One Drop & Rockers
lines for the in utero-trance-mission.*

*'Check the teeth of the sound. Will it bite?
Muscles... how does it k/not?' LEFIFI and his
drums. Dashiki spear-burn. MALOMBO Jazz-
men & makers. Julian Bahula. We are percussive,
here, at home. What difference but the spirit
blowing the cattle in. Kraaling. 'We are the
elephant' – rhythm tattooing the Afrikaland.*

*MAX ROACHING it West African to raise the
sun back in cold Apacheland. Decimation of its
bloodbeats. Getting a tenth off. Tithes to the gods
left back in the Drum-motherland. Some have no
knowledge of the age: 'play the drums' can mean
'give out bursaries... in free arse-whuppings'... cos
percussion is born also on bed-rock, & sea-shells,
following close on chains around smashed wrists.*

*'The Creator Has a Master-Plan'
Got the quill dipped in a Black Star for the ink.
Wrote it across the firmament.
That is why the Jazz goes Free out into space in
search.*

SUN RA riding through the universe on a
Repatriation-rhythm.

BIRD was so great, I heard that mistakes he
made... on record... other players are still getting
that shit rehearsed... itching to get the errors
perfect.

No 'cuss-cuss' to my brothers & sisters in the
Americas... flavour of the jam that is the gore on
the Atlantic floor. Salt-water over bone sounds.
Like how the cordite-wave against black bodies
pounds, might be lark & shark opposite but the
effect is the same: obliteration!

Bermuda triangle sucks up & mangles sound,
senses fallen into the vortex. Bird-line. Hope at the
end of the rope. Swirl & whirl, the trill & the jar,
thrills & fears. Single file or packed in multiple
chords.

Not bubbles he blows time pro-spirit, is capsules
not anti-body... (I re-phrase on the rebound)
Ancient romance memory present disharmony but
his playing is transport out. Call of the galaxies.
But them, the blabber-preachers laying lines
elementary like 'She is a baby making factory &
he a dick in torn overalls just walking & talking,
no, rocking and spurting...'

MZWANDILE BUTHELEZI gave me an art-work opposite anaemia. Red paint of black. 'Blacks look so good when they bleed' some Caucasoid photojournalist told Santu Mofokeng, handing in pics for the day's spread. Black man in the gutter dying. Snapped, like his neck at impossible angle. Mzwandile's piece like a bit of flesh come off back of the head, close to the jugular, no, that split open & the corpuscles scattering out – fingers of callous labour plucking barbed wire bowing to upright bass-strings... (to pull the guys out of the wood, not to prostrate, get it right) sparks & blood flying off wood & metal in all directions, getting out, escaped slave-notes.

... & the beast of rebellion has come loose, off the madding machine. Look, first it was freed off the tree & now... from it gets liberated... SOUND! When I saw it I knew a LIVE THING. The wood breathing. Getting hurt? More like doing the hurting. Pain in there, deep. Regardless. Giving or taking, no matter. From whom to where the HARM?

The Mothers of Invention were ecstatic over what they had laid down. Smiling proudly when Zappa walked in. They got it played back to him. He listened, & then tore the whole thing down, saying it was too... beautiful.

An earlier time, a different place. The band had rehearsed six tunes, were ready to lay tracks down, some takes. Bird walked in, stood around, listened, walked out, never to return. Later he was asked why he'd abandoned the session. He said: 'It was just too beautiful... i couldn't...'

I hide in here against the humans getting pulped beyond these walls. For company 2 potatoes, 1 garlic clove, 1 onion, 2 tomatoes, 2 peppers, 1 cabbage. 1 5-litre bottled water. 2.5kg mielie meal, 1 250ml pre-used vegetable oil, 1 salt shaker. 1 stale half-loaf white bread. 6 empty green beer bottles in the corner. A small plastic bag containing a number of cigarette stubs. A two-plate electric stove, rusted so the white it originally was is spotted with brown-black blotches. The one plate no longer works. The working one is jammed at one heat-speed. A melamine-topped two-door, half-sized kitchen cabinet, chipped in several places. A built-in concrete sink. Three beat pots, different sizes, the one lacking a lid. A pan. A single coir mattress nestling in the corner, 3 blankets, 2 frayed, threadbare dish-rags. The house itself used to be allocated to railway workers, train-drivers, to be exact, for lay-overs. Solid brown structure a metre above the water-mark. The roof leaks in places, the pelmet creaks in the wind. The paint that runs for half-a-metre down from the roof has been peeling off for years now.

These complete my housing arrangements. In this community i am rich. My books do not enter the equation. My 3 pants 5 shirts 3 of them tees, my

1 pair of running fake-leather black shoes, don't either. Like the trees clustered around the place, all corners, moving in. A veritable bush. They are old & gnarled, the trees. Branches resembling zombie-skeletons with their limbs drooping near liquid, at night. Eyes cast down, not looking at the world but trying to get within, into the soul. To eat a hole through the chest & bury the head inside. Sad looking vegetation, here. I gaze at the scene just once in the morning, upon waking & quickly look away before the trees spot me. Feel Peeping Tommish, shameful. Staring at the trees showing their unwashed nakedness. Cousin to the Kgalagadi desert, this place. Kin to the arid.

At the shop a white customer speaks to the assistant, black male. The assistant nods, vigorously, walks through a door & into a back room. He is gone for a couple of minutes. The white man stands there, hand on hips, humming some tune. The assistant re-appears carrying a wrapped package. The other assistant, also black blurts out, top of his voice: 'You there, Spencer, when a white man sends you to do something, you must run.' The shopkeeper, hitting the till, chuckles, pleased, exchanging looks with the customer. He jackals his face in a wide grin. He mutters: 'Kaffirs, man!' He is Indian. The white man giggles, cuts it short.

I stand there, gagging. Their deal done, i walk
up to Spencer, standing there eyes angled at the
floor, become an embarrassed child. I am looking
for batteries, greet him, he doesn't respond, i wait
a while, then ask him where the batteries are to
be found. He raises his eyes. Shame turned to
disgust all over his face. Looks me up & down like
i'm some object of repulsion... & walks off, leaving
me standing there. Shopkeeper, other assistant,
customer gathering his things off the counter, all
pretend i don't exist.

I have heard black customers get insults, their
mothers' genitals, their fathers' impotent scrota,
hurled at them as if it was normalcy. & the
customers take it. I walk to the door, turn, stand
there, stare at each of them, look at the clock on
the wall, 15 minutes to closing, & walk out, sit
on the stoep, & wait for lock-up time. Someone
is not going to sleep well for the next couple of
days. I have seen in the municipal offices, police
stations, all governmental buildings, hospitals, at
the supermarkets, how the bow & scrape works
across skin-colour, how prostrate tongues push
lips apart into sickly grins at sight of whiteness.

Flip that coin, have Black stand there & watch
the phantom vomit take flight at their face across
the till-machine. How Black demean Black. At
the bank, in restaurants, waiters giving the

impression they deem it beneath them to be serving one pigmented like them. Airport security officers wrinkling their noses like Blacks smell. Black policemen brutalising their people with greater savagery if a white fellow grunting pig be in attendance. It wells up in me, i have heard it said without any irony that 'the greatest black is lower than the lowest of the worst white'.

The lava of it bubbles, threatens to spew out, i swallow it back and push it onto my forearms. Telling it 'Patience, later... for now... we sit. No ambush, they have to see it coming. I want to be VISIBLE when they get to the door to close & lock it. Know i am waiting. I will not hide in the undergrowth on their way home. No, we do it here. The minutes will pass. & they will come out...'

The clock in my head ticks. The fuse starts burning. En route to the psycho-dynamite. Adrenalin surge pumps close to bursting. It is not angry blackman time. All rage is collected, stored deep.

I pick up a heavy rusted metal pipe leaning against the wall, sit on the stoep, & wait. Knowing the pipe will not break but the brain-cells will get working on with it, much inspired as a result of the contact-sport. Head-split. Crack so air gets in, cool the brain to proper thought.

To distil decades' pen-rage. Drop one line more powerful than an entire novel. Have Fikile, Dumile & Thami live here.